MW00936582

WHERE ISLANDS ARE

By:

M.D. Mynhier

TO My new friend, Laura
I wish you the best
and hope you've already
found your perfect Island!
        your friend
        M D My—l
        8/11/18

This book is for

ELSA, MY ISLAND GIRL

While breezes off the sea bring a good feeling to some, those same breezes stir in others, a need to see from where they came.

M.D. Mynhier

The sun was tilting toward the horizon as we made Key West, so our first stop was a bed and breakfast on Duval Street where we hustled our bags to the room and hurriedly tossed them on the bed. Being in a rush to get this life going, we left our room straight away and walked to the end of the street, arriving at Mallory Square as the sun dipped deep and the Sunset Festival was full on. We stopped and ate conch fritters that I'd dickered the price with from a street vendor as fire-eaters, escape artist, and Jimmy Buffett impersonators were raking in buckets of tips and we sashayed among the tourists finding our place by absorbing native vibes. Since we were of the newest native tribe, assimilation was key to acceptance in this strange land.

My island girl and I had moved to Key West with a loosely formed plan to sail the Caribbean for all we were worth, we had a fair plan, though a little risky but I have always felt, what good is an adventure without it being somewhat dicey? After all, Ernest Hemingway, Harry Truman and Jimmy Buffett found Key West alluring to one's rowdier side. It's where creativity flows and individualism is treasured most above all else. I was steeped in wishes that some island magic remained and could nibble its way into our souls. At this point, I didn't care if it was voodoo magic that made it fun as long as it wasn't my chicken or goat!

Now that the kids had grown-up and moved-on with families and relationships of their own leaving a deep void in their wake, it was go for the gold time or never for us. We had spent our dime and bought a big ass sailboat large enough to live on and were going to let the waves rock us to sleep every night. Our boat was supposed to arrive in Key West any day and I couldn't wait. I pictured holding my island girl close, drifting off

to sleep as the boat slowly swayed and sea breezes cooling the night with us lying in

the darkness listening to distant ship's bells sound while waves lap lightly against the hull and waking to dolphin pods arcing from the sea and gulls gliding a sunrise.

My dream was one that in the cool of early morning, I'll sip coffee and click words out on the laptop as writers tend to do while my island girl sits on-deck reading or snapping photographs while waiting for the sun to rise high. We'll both be ready for a swim with the late morning heat. Later, we may go into town for some shopping or take her out for a short sail or maybe all the way to Marathon Key or to Key Largo for a few days. Some mornings, we'll just sail out of land's sight into the Gulf Stream.

On the days we sail out into the Gulf Stream, I'll fish for marlin, sailfish, grouper and tuna while my island girl sunbathes and photographs birds of all kinds doing her thing as she pleases. We'll just spend days at a time catering each other's desires. With plenty food and drink stored in the galley, there will be no reason to hurry back to port. The Island Girl will be our tropical island and we'll live as the last couple on earth doing as we please answering only to our personal inhibitions.

All of this was a long drive, and a long way from the hills of Kentucky but we were excited seeing Brown Pelicans perched on pilings and gulls sailing as white specks against a blue gulf waters. I was having a blast watching the expressions on my girl's face change as she looked to the bluest of waters dotted with boats and families swimming off small islands. Every scene was a postcard waiting to happen. This was it. We were doing it and we squeezed each other's hand tighter with each step we took.

This was our big adventure and we had waited a long time for it. What we were doing was scary, maybe even a little crazy and at the same time thrilling. We were taking our chance. Seeing her eyes light up and her wide smile was well worth it.

This night on the island was ours to enjoy. With luck, there would be many more. Tomorrow, or the day after, our boat should make port. I'd hired a captain from up north to sail her from where I had purchased her in Lake Erie. He was sailing her to Key West by himself. She was an eighty-footer with tall sails and all the technology a modern day sailor could want. But now, the island was whispering in my ear to feast, dance and play the entire town with my island girl until dawn then take her to the seaside for the sunrise.

Our first stop was at Sloppy Joe's, where I bought a Hemingway hatpin for luck and then we eased over to Captain Tony's and from there to The Hog's Breath Saloon. We had a few drinks, danced, laughed and watched all the action and the strange people that seemed to be at home here on the island, and then we headed to find a bite to eat. We settled on the Grand Café where we sat on the veranda and beneath candlelight ate the best blackened mahi mahi on the island.

After we had eaten, we took in the sights. The air was very warm and humid and the smell of the sea on the air intoxicating. The moon weaved through thin white clouds and wide leaves of palms. The broad leaves of Banana trees slowly stirred in the slight breezes as we walked toward the pier. Lights from a docked cruise ship looked like a tall building at a distance. It was all new to us and we were loving it as the night swiftly passed into morning.

We had walked in the predawn to secluded area of beach arriving at the sea's edge as sunrise came over a long point filled with bent crooked palm trees curling their way toward the sky. As we clung to each other, the yellows and oranges of the new sun jabbed between jagged palm fronds flashing into the blue water with colors of lightening and molted lava. The sea stirred as if batting its eyes from the brightness and awakening with a yawn of long stretching waves. We sat on the white sand not flinching for fear it would all go away.

I have no idea how long we sat on that beach but it was such a spectacular vision I never wanted us to leave. I now knew what had drawn Hemingway and Buffett to this place. I could only imaging as we sat there how a sunrise could be from the deck of The Island Girl far out in the gulf where we would be all the sun had to dazzle. But I did know we would certainly love it. There was nothing to not love here.

Down the beach, an old man in khaki shorts and a beat-up straw hat walked across white sand towards the sea carrying a metal bucket and a fishing rod. He was stringy with skin dark as old leather. When near the surf, he sat the bucket upside down on the beach and took a tackle-pack off his shoulder placing it on the sand. He sat on the bucket, tied a lure to the line, stood and started casting. With little effort, he sent the lure a great distance through the air out into the surf and I admired his skill.

We walked closely by him as we were leaving the beach to chase down breakfast. He glanced back at us once to see if we were in his way. His eyes were as blue as the sea and seemed in a permanent squint from looking into the sun glair off the sea. I think he looked older than he was and had that toughness about him of a retired warrior that had fought more than his share of battles.

As we entered a café, I couldn't get him off my mind. It was the way he looked at us that had my attention. There was something soothing about his eyes. Maybe he was just a loner happy with where he was and with what he was doing and was glad we were leaving. He looked like he had earned the right to do whatever he wanted. I hoped that I would meet him again and we'd have the opportunity to become friends.

The café was an old 1800's two-story house with a second floor balcony overlooking a large tropical garden and the street. We asked for a balcony table and we were seated overlooking a garden leading to the street. A ship's anchor was the centerpiece of the garden. It was huge and pitted badly from hundreds of years beneath the sea. We ordered coffee and blueberry pancakes and the morning street now alive with colorful people going out for breakfast too.

As we ate, we decided go to the Mel Fisher museum and see the silver and gold recovered from sunken Spanish galleons. The blueberry pancakes were stuffed with a filling of very rich blueberry cream cheese and the first bite awoke every taste bud in my mouth. We ate, drank coffee and people-watched from the balcony most of the morning. Later we walked to Mel Fisher's and the Pirate museum.

We had been up all night and after the museums; we went back to our room, showered and grabbed a mid-day nap. It was the heat of the day and all good pirates took siestas to escape the heat and to ready themselves for a night on the town. In a sense, we were pirates waiting on our ship to arrive and sleep came easy as the ceiling fan slowly turned, hypnotizing us into deep slumber. If I dreamed, I don't remember.

When I awoke, it was late afternoon and the sun had passed the midday peak. I lay watching the blades of the ceiling fan, feeling the air brush over my body. My Island girl looked peaceful, I watched her breathing, and it was in harmony with the slow turning fanblades. I eased out of bed and lit a smoke. I was feeling hungry and thirsty, mostly thirsty, and wanting my boat to hurry on in. I slipped out of the room to get us food and drink leaving her asleep.

The plaza down the street was stirring with activity and I noticed a seafood shack at the rear of the food court and ordered shrimp and rice for two, island style, and two large sweet iced teas, to go. As I waited, a man began setting-up shop at a table between shops. He was selling hand rolled cigars and made one as I watched. When I passed-by him with my take-out order, he grinned and offered-up a free cigar he'd just rolled.

I accepted the cigar and chatted with him. After a few moments, he showed me a wooden humidor he said was filled with the finest Cuban cigars. There were twenty-four cigars and he wanted $250.00 for them. I told him they may well be worth the price, but that I wouldn't know the difference between Cuban cigars and a box of King Edwards. I thanked him for the free smoke and headed for the room. A troupe of free ranging Key West chickens darted across the street in front of me stopping traffic until they were safely in a yard.

My island girl awakened while I was gone and had showered and dressed for an evening out. We ate in a hurry not wanting to miss the fun that would soon start along Duval Street and Mallory Square. As we arrived at the square, a clipper ship was entering the bay. Its sleek tall sails were a masterpiece against the sky. Crewmembers scurried as passengers waved toward shore. Seeing her sailing into port made me want The Island Girl here and now.

We looked on as the clipper docked and then we walked around checking out the street performers. One escape artist, handcuffed, wrapped in chains and hanging upside down from a tall tripod shouted out like a carnival barker to passersby as tourist gathered to watch him attempt his escape. I had never seen a man more secured, his entire body was wrapped tightly in heavy chain and padlocked with his hands cuffed behind his back. Once a sufficient crowd had gathered and were pitching money in his bucket, he asked, "Would you be surprised if I were able to free myself in less than one minute?" There were murmurs throughout the crowd and one very drunk man that had recently disembarked from a cruise ship said, "I'd be surprised and amazed if you could masturbate right now! By god, I'd pay to see something like that." The crowd laughed and we watched as he shucked the chains and handcuffs and landed back on the ground feet first and smiling all the way to the bank. He gathered the bucket of money and readied his show for the next cruise ship group to disembark.

Later in the night, we headed off to the marina. I wanted to check with the harbormaster on the status of The Island Girl. The harbormaster was a dry sort but I did I learn from him that he had had radio communication with my boat and it would be in tomorrow evening at the latest. We decided to charter a fishing trip for the following morning because fishing passes time in a good way.

We ate oysters and shrimp as a midnight dinner and turned in early as island time goes. The next morning, we met the captain of the fishing boat we'd chartered at the dock. He was a young colorful fellow, barefoot and only wearing shorts. I yelled, "Permission to come aboard?"

He said, "Stay off my goddamn boat," as he made his way to us holding a water hose. He said, "Turn your shoes up and I'll wash them off. I want no sand, shit or assholes in my boat."

I thought it was too late for the asshole part, figuring he had been aboard many times. I started to tell him where he could stick his boat, but he laughed and said after hosing our shoe bottoms, "Now come aboard," I wasn't sure how this was going to go, but my nature is to plow forward. I stepped into his boat and said, "You don't mind it if I pull slimy-ass fish aboard your "goddamn" boat do you?"

He laughed and said, "I like fish, its assholes that tend to piss me off."

I threw a sideways glance his way, laughed and said, "Yeah, me too."

I got the bowline and he the stern. In a minute, we were headed fifteen miles closer to Cuba. We had calm seas in the bay but a headwind outside the cover of the island made for a choppy ride. Once out, he checked the GPS guiding us to where he thought we should start and there he dropped anchor.

I looked all around and It all looked the same so I asked, "Why this spot?"

He said, "We're over a wreck." I got his drift, as I took a rod he handed me and baited the hook with what looked like a big bluegill from the livebait-well.

I cast the bait as far as I could and let it free-spool with my thumb lightly touching on the live as it spun until it hit bottom. It didn't take long for the pole to bend. The fight was on. I fought the fish about ten minutes and still had a ways to go when something big hit my fish and it was on. The drag was singing and I couldn't slow it. "What the hell?" I said.

The captain answered, "Big goddamn tiger shark just ate your fish. Hang on. I'll fire up the big motor and go after it."

He followed and I reeled line hoping to land my first tiger shark. Every nerve I had was tingling. My forearms were on fire but I was determined to get this fish. He would make runs and then I'd gain line back and he'd run again taking the line I'd gotten. This went for an hour and I had him hooked good. My island girl was nervous too. She wiped streams of sweat from my face and eyes with a towel and asked me if I was okay. I was working hard, but hell, I was great.

We chased the shark and I was putting a death pressure on him reeling down lifting the rod tip up and reeling down again. I was gaining line pumping the rod and gaining more for over an hour and a half I fought this fish and then, the line, it just popped and there was nothing. I handed the rod to the captain and then sat in the fighting chair. Wiping sweat from my face on my shirtfront, I said, "Rig it to go again." I glanced at my island girl and from her smile I knew we were home.

The captain said, 'Fucking shark", as he tied a new hook and got up from the fighting chair and dipped another baitfish. When we got back to the wreck, he said, "If you get your ass pulled overboard, don't bother coming back aboard unless you've still got my pole."

I said, "It'll take a hell of a fish to jerk my ass out of the boat."

He said, "By-god they're here."

My island girl was taking it all in. She knew my hard ass stance and was ready to watch the show.

I let go a good cast and asked him, "How'd you come to captain a fishing boat?" Before he answered, I said, "Let me guess, your great people skills and shining personality lead you to it?"

He laughed and said, "It don't bother you a goddamn, does it? You're not one bit scared."

I looked him in the eyes and said, "Hell, I was raised around guns, whiskey and mean ass hillbilly bootleggers. But that's okay. I'm paying for a good show too.

Just then, the pole bent and I set the hook. We had hit on a school of grouper and within an hour, I had ten nice ones in the boat. My island girl had spent most of the morning photographing birds, me, and the grouper as I pulled them in. The sun peaked signaling lunch-time and we headed back to the dock and a bite to eat. As we entered the bay, a dolphin leaped and twirled near the boat as my island girl snapped pictures. She was having a great time.

We took our captain to lunch because, as I told my island girl, he looked hungry and may yet have something nice to say to someone. And if so, I wanted to be on hand to hear it. He scowled at my words and I never let on. My island girl knew me only too well and smiled at my gouging him. We were on dry land, well sort of. It was a floating dock and not his boat. It was my turn now. She wished I wouldn't, but knew better.

"So, ever force a charter to walk the plank?" I asked. Before he answered, I followed with, "Bet you've keel hauled a few helpless fishermen in your day?"

He said, "I wish I had of done another one this morning."

I took the menu, ordered drinks, and chose the one with the sissyest sounding name listed and ordered it for him. I knew that would blister his ass when the waitress served it to him instead of my island girl.

The drinks arrived, the waitress handed him the sissy drink and grinned. He took it, looked into it, grabbed the little umbrella from it and sailed it across the room, produced a flask from his shorts pocket, dumped rum into the drink, then turned the flask up and took a big slug and chased it with the drink I'd bought, slamming the empty glass down without ever letting on. I ordered another for him then I guzzled his flask empty.

My island girl looked on and no words were spoken as more drinks arrived. The waitress gave him his sissy drink. He held up the empty flask. The waitress retrieved it, took it to the bar and filled it. I should have seen this coming, I thought to myself. We were on his home water. He poured the sissy drink into the table's centerpiece bouquet of tropical flowers, filled his glass from the flask and gulped it down.

About that time, our food arrived and we ate in silence knowing the one whom spoke first, lost. In mid meal, I signaled the waitress for another round. Our captain pushed his cute little drink aside and continued to drink from his flask. My island girl was nibbling on her fruit salad and sipping iced tea. I had oysters on the half shell. The captain had the same. After about an hour, he said. "Let's shove off."

I needed to check with the Harbor Master on my boat and told the captain so. He said that we could contact The Island Girl from his boat while we were headed out to fish. I had only hired him for a morning trip and reminded him of that. He said, "It's on me cause I can't keep my trap shut." I grinned to myself as we made way. Stopping short of going aboard, I waited on the water hose and the foot washing ceremony.

My island girl decided to stay ashore and shop while we fished the evening away. We agreed to meet at Sloppy Joe's around dark. I gave her a kiss as my shoes were being hosed-off. Captain Jack Sparrow, as I now called him just to piss him off, was a bit tipsy and washed my shoe bottoms, legs and my crotch when the boat was rocked by a wave. We agreed to have a drink then cast off. We both took a pull from his flask.

He said, "I have more in the ship's hold."

I was feeling no pain either and thought it comical to address him as Captain Jack. He didn't seem to mind so I dug in to pursue other measures to irritate him. We were soon out of the bay and the twin 200-horse engines were rolling a long wake. We drank and bounced across waves that were almost constant at this speed. "Where are we going?" I asked.

"Cuba. Havana Harbor. I want some Cuban," he never finished the sentence as he cut sharply to miss an oncoming boat. And I didn't care what Cuban thing he wanted.

It was a straight shot from Key West to Havana. I figured he was full of shit and I wasn't sure where we were going. I was fairly certain it was against the law to go to Cuba, but what the hell, Hemingway and rum runners made the trip all the time, I thought, as I took another nip from the flask. "Hey wait a minute," I yelled. "I want to fish and my island girl is not going to be happy with me calling her from a Cuban slammer."

He said, "Don't worry, by god I'll have you back in time for drinks and dinner." I still wasn't sure where Captain Jack was headed, but I did know that with a couple more pulls from the flask I wouldn't care. I had memorized all the stories of rum running and everyone wants a real hand rolled Cuban cigar hanging from his lips.

"What the hell." I said, "Let's go to Havana!" I knew I wasn't too drunk when I realized I couldn't speak a single syllable of Cuban.

A dialogue about "the baseball" kept running through my mind and "The great DiMaggio." All I wanted to do was catch the great fish and be lucky. But here I was getting drunk with Captain Jack busting ass across the ocean and headed for a prison or worse in Havana. Fidel could shoot us as spies. On the other hand, he may have a soft spot for two drunken fishermen just out bucking the system. After all, it was American law we were breaking, not Cuban. Hell, Castro would like that.

The sky was as blue as the sea and with no land in sight; whatever we were doing was getting ready to happen soon and I needed to get drunker before it did.

"Hey Jack Sparrow, the goddamned Cuban navy is going to sink us I'll wager." Yes, I was sure that we were going to soon die somewhere off the coast of Havana long before we could make our pitch to Castro. "Reckon we'll make the TV news on the mainland?" I said.

"I have never ever been caught in Havana Harbor."

"Well, how many times you done it?"

Captain Jack acted as if I had not posed that question and said, "Take the wheel. I'll get more rum," as he turned loose and walked away I grabbed the wheel and held a somewhat steady course.

Jack popped back up from the hold with a bottle in his hand and another underneath his arm and I figured what the hell, getting drunker was the thing with where we were headed. I knew my island girl was going to be pissed as a wet hen even though she had seen me do silly ass things like this for years. Every time, I think she thought I had learned my lesson. But to me, each one was a new crazy deed and I always had to learn the hard way. This would be close to the granddaddy of them all.

Jack passed me the bottle. I turned it up, took a good pull, and handed it back as I quivered. "Stout stuff," I said.

When he pulled the bottle from his lips, he said, "It'll cure shark bites, crabs and make ugly bow-legged women look pretty damned good in the dark."

I said, "Hell, give me some more. I haven't seen much that works on ugly women other than paper bags. Ever think of putting this stuff on the market? It'll sell for sure!

Do they drink it or do you rub it on them, or both? How's it work on them?"

He handed me the bottle and said, "I am not sure how it works best. I usually just drink a shit load of it and it does the job. You need to save some for the next morning though, just in case they get too pretty in the night and you forget to leave before first light."

I thought about it a moment and said, "You drink it and they get better looking, a strange way of working?" I took another drink and said, "We got to market this juice because it's got me seeing land dead ahead."

Captain Jack grabbed the wheel too late and we hit the beach wide open and shot about 100 yards up the sand between two big dunes. I swung my head around in all directions and couldn't see the ocean anywhere. We were hidden from the sea by dunes and tall sea oats sprouting all about. I took two big swallows of the rum, handed the bottle to Jack, and asked, "Will this shit get us back in the water as easy as it got us out of it?"

He considered my question a moment and said, " Well, mate, it got us out of it, so it should work both ways as I figure."

"You think we're in Cuba?" I was ready to charge San Juan Hill or any place else just as soon as we drank all the rum and got the boat turned around and pointed back to sea. "You know," I said, "This boat drove itself up here; I figure it'll drive itself back if we get it turned. How much of this juice do you think we have?" Captain Jack was scratching his head and had a puzzled look to him.

"I think we missed Cuba, myself," I said.

"And why do you think we've missed Cuba?" He said.

"Because I think I just saw a big ass Puerto Rican cockroach run into those weeds, as I pointed to a thick patch of tall grass, "and this stuff don't work on cockroaches because it was still damned ugly."

He handed me the bottle and said, "You just haven't drank enough to make cockroaches pretty, However you are close to the making ugly women pretty stage, but still far from the cockroach's being pretty stage." I took his word and downed more rum.

As I put the bottle to my lips, it hit me. My island girl was going to be damned mad. My only way out was to make this all Jack's fault. Captain Jack was surveying the damage, cursing rum and taking a slug from a second bottle.

I yelled to him, "You have any friends with boats?" He must have had to think about it because he didn't answer quickly.

"Yeah, I have a friendly mate or two with boats," he finally said.

"Well," I said. "Why don't you get on the horn and call them for help?"

"Good idea," He said.

I asked, "Where in the hell are we?"

He took another pull of rum squinted one eye as he carefully surveyed the area, and said, "I believe we're most likely on a goddamn island."

That was not what I had wanted to hear but I agreed. He was right. I jumped out of the boat into the hot sand and walked up and over the rim of the island. There were a few palms, a beach and the sea. It was a miniature island with boaters tied-off and swimming all around the far side. I yelled back to Jack, "Cuba's a little ass island, huh?"

He walked up to where I was and took a gander. "We'll requisition two of those vessels. That will be the key to pulling us off the beach."

I was enjoying taking pot shots at Jack. I said, "We going to steal them like real pirates? Hell, I'm in! Highjacking Cuban boats is a great idea. They probably stole them from Americans to start with. Is that Havana Harbor we're looking' at? I really had Cuba pictured as a bigger place."

He took another drink, looked at me and said, "This is not the goddamned island of Cuba dumbass."

I was trying to keep a straight face when I said, "You're the Captain, Jack, I was assured we were on a course for Havana Harbor and figured you had us on course and we were there."

Jack turned up the bottle, took a good whack, and said, "You go tell them of our terrible misfortune and despicable situation."

I looked him in the eye and said, "You do it, Jack. You got us here. Dumbass."

Then, I thought about it a second and said, "Let's go together. We'll take rum and after a few they'll understand."

He was on-board with that, and said, "By god, you are a thinker."

I pointed to my temple and said, "By god, it's all up here. You just let me do the thinking" We started downhill towards the beach to where the swimmers were.

Jack stopped and said, "Hang on," as he headed back to our boat. A few minutes later, he came back with four more bottles of rum.

"They are going to love us." I said," as we headed through the sand over the topknot of the island to the little beach.

"They sure are," he said, "Free party and all they must to do is swing around the island and pull us off."

I was having a hell of a time and couldn't wait until I shared this story with buddies. I knew my island girl wasn't going to see too much humor in it, but a tale like this is a once in a lifetime.

"Rum for all," I yelled as we made the far beach.

They looked at us kind of weird and I turned to Jack and asked, "Reckon they speak English? You know any Cuban, just in case?"

Jack stopped in his tracks as if pondering my questions, and then he said, "There is no such thing as speaking Cuban. Cubans speak goddamn Mexican."

I looked at him and said, "It would sound better if Mexicans spoke Cuban. Or maybe mix them up together and have them all speak Cubican? Yep, I like that idea."

"What the hell?" Jack said.

"I'm inventing the way to change the world. It's common knowledge that Arizona and most of North America dislike Mexicans but don't seem to have anything against Cubans. If Mexicans spoke Cubican, then they'd be Cubicans and not Mexicans. Get my drift. We can change it all by renaming the country Cubico and have them all speaking Cubican. Give me some more rum and I'll have it all worked out in an hour or two. Jack, you get the boat. I got this. "

Having just invented a wonderful new language and founded a new nation, I figured I was on a roll. The only worry I had was what my island girl would do because of this. I had to come up with a plan. I needed a good one too. She would never buy that we were drunk and ran the boat aground on a little island somewhere in the Caribbean, between Key West and Cuba. It's always a bad deal when the truth sounds too farfetched to believe.

I decided on being honest. She deserved the truth and it was the only way I could tell the story later without getting in trouble. We needed to get this boat off the beach and head her back to Key West. She would be waiting at Sloppy Joe's and by god I was not going to disappoint her. "Hey Jack, let's get a move on. A very pretty lady is waiting on me and I'm going to be there."

He looked up and said, "Where?"

"At Sloppy Joe's." I said.

He answered, "What's at Sloppy Joe's?"

I was drunk, but he was wasted. A crowd gathered and Jack passed around the rum. He turned and said, "Arrr mate, we have found our crew."

"Shit, Jack, we need to get the boat from dry dock. We need help and you're turning it into a party."

"You hear that?" He said. "We're having a party to celebrate. Hell, I don't really know what we're celebrating. But I'm in."

"Jack, are they going to help us?"

"I assure you we have a pleasant crew of unruly mates here and at hand. And after a few drams of rum, we'll attend to the displeasure of work. As you know, this is a serious situation and demands considerable thought before prescribing to any action" He was becoming Captain Jack Sparrow before my eyes. By calling him Captain Jack as a joke, I had created a monster.

I was feeling no pain but Jack was out of control. He was having a big time with the attention he gained from handing out free rum. The ladies were brown and had little on and were quite friendly as native islanders go. I had a feeling this would have a bad ending and wanted out as soon as possible. At best, I was in for a royal ass chewing when we got back. At worst, we could get our asses beat silly by the guys with the almost naked native girls.

"Jack, we need to make sail. The entire state of Cubico is in limbo and we are its only hope."

He took another drink from the bottle and said, "You hear that mates? We have a state to save and a world to change and shouldn't keep it waiting. Bring your ships about and we'll dislodge my vessel." They followed his orders for some crazy reason. I took a pull from my bottle to be on the safe side, figuring at this point sober man wouldn't make sense.

We tied off to the bow of Jack's boat and to the two boats and they counted down and went full throttle. Our boat turned in the sand and slid into the sea slick as if greased. "By god there Jack, you did it." I said.

He smiled and said, "Of course, we have business to attend to now in Cubico."

I nodded and said, "It'll have to wait until tomorrow. We have to make sail for Sloppy Joe's and save a damsel in distress."

Jack rubbed his chin and said, "If it weren't for what we must do, we could do so much more of what we should do." I nodded again, but I needed to think about this one. Either, I was really drunk, or Jack was starting to sound smarter than he looked. He hit the key, the engines fired, coughed a few times, and settled into a normal rhythm.

"Which way is Key West, Jack?" He pointed, then switched his point ever so slightly until he had pointed everywhere on the map.

As far as I knew, we were still headed to Cuba. Jack had damaged the electronic instruments when we ran aground and nothing worked.

"Navigation by the stars is how America was discovered," He said.

I didn't have to think about this one, "Hell, Jack, the suns high in the sky. There are no stars."

He never skipped a beat, "There will be before this is over. All my charts and compass was on this screen that don't work anymore."

"So which way, Jack?"

He pondered a moment and said, "We go where the sun was."

He was drunk and had no clue. All I wanted was to get back to Key West before dark. I could see her wearing a new island dress looking as pretty as any gal on Duval Street waiting for me in front of Sloppy Joe's. And I was not going to disappoint her. I looked at Jack and said, "Listen up shithead, I have a date and we are going in now. You got that?"

He said, "There will be no threats of mutiny on a vessel of mine."

I said, "You're too drunk to think. I'll get us in. You take a rest and sober up. Then we'll talk." He sat in the fighting chair, strapped himself in and was soon slumped and snoring. I put a cap on him to shade him from the sun a bit and set a course as near due East as I could, keeping the sun over my left shoulder. I hit full throttle and we were ricocheting, skipping waves like a flat rock skimming across a creek.

After about thirty minutes, I seen fishing boats on the horizon and made for them with hopes they were out of Key West. I knew this late in the day boats would be heading to port. All I had to do was follow. It's somewhat like being bewildered in the hills back home. Just use your head, listen for sounds of log trucks or distant barking of a hound, follow it and walk your way out using your head and not walking in circles.

I steered behind a shrimper keeping a safe distance while following his lead. I wasn't positive the course was for Key West, but we were headed into a port somewhere. My inter compass told me we were going east and that made sense. Captain Jack was still slumped in the fighting chair past out cold. I was sobering up and feeling nauseated about the trouble I was going to be in if I didn't get where I needed to be on time.

I don't want to paint the wrong picture of my island girl. She is as sweet as they get and I love her dearly, but like anyone, when expecting to be met at a certain time, she wants to be met. Now, if I were held up by weather, or by fighting a giant fish, she'd more than understand. But, if being late is because of getting drunk and running the boat aground, I cannot picture her as being a happy camper.

About the same time land came into sight, Jack started coming around. He moaned and kicked a bit, then said, "Where's the rum. I tell you, I need the hair of the dog. To swim with the sharks, you must stay a shark." I didn't bother looking back. At this point, I really didn't give a damn if he dumped overboard. Part of the blame was mine, I guess. I started the drinking at lunch to get the best of Jack.

"Jack, we're headed in." He couldn't stand, but managed to reach a bottle and was following the hair of the dog philosophy, plucking a hair at a time.

He pulled the bottle from his lips and said, "Run ashore, I'll claim the new land in the name of our new nation, Cubico, home to all good pirates and sex starved maidens. Do you have a Cubican flag to plant deep into her soil?"

I yelled, "Hell, Jack, I don't even know what the Cubican flag should look like."

Jack attempted to rise but fell and crawled forward into the hold. I heard him scrambling and banging as wave action bounced his drunken ass around. I was hoping he was out of rum, but should have known better. I had come to understand that Jack was a good sailor but when drunk, a terrible captain of a fishing charter. He was resilient and lucky. Both traits are most admirable in men, but he was also as nuts as I'd ever seen.

One moment he washes your shoe soles to keep sand out of the boat, next moment, he's rammed the boat onto a sand covered beach, then drinks a toast to being somewhere between dry-docked and shipwrecked as he wallows barefoot and drunk beside the boat yelling, "Jump in, the sand is great." My island girl wasn't going to believe one word of this unless Captain Jack tells it to her himself. She needs to see him to believe it.

Now I had a plan. Taking Jack with me to meet-up with my island girl was brilliant. She would have to understand then. "Jack, what the hell you doing down there?" I yelled. All I heard was thumping and knocking about. Jack was my ace in the hole and I had to keep him somewhat safe for my own well-being. She was sure to be proud that I was tough enough to make it back alive. She was going to really love me for it.

Jack mumbled something inaudible while he kept rumbling around the hold. In a few minutes he emerged with an old army duffle and a cloth with a picture of a black seal balancing a ball on its nose, and the words, Black Seal Rum, and a Jolly Mon tee shirt, he began to cut and tear with a filleting knife. I watched, wondering what the hell he was up to. Then he grabbed a box containing sewing needles and fishing line.

"Will you stop this goddamned boat? I'm making the Cubican flag. A man can't do shit bouncing all over the place." He yelled.

"No. If I stop, we'll be late. And by god, I'm making landfall before dark. What the hell are you doing anyway?"

"I told you, I'm creating the flag of Cubico and this is my vessel and you'll set her dead in the water or I'll be forced to shoot your ass," he said, as he pulled an old pistol from a storage compartment.

"Goddamnit Jack, put that thing down before it goes off and you blow a hole in the boat or worse." Jack was failing that old pistol around over his head and looking like some nut from a crazy house. He said, "We're heading for Cubico to pillage the land then claim it for ourselves. We'll crown your woman the Queen of Cubico and you King. As long as I am commander of the Cubican navy, you can have the land."

"Where is this Cubico anyway?" I asked.

"That's a tricky question, mate. But all that matters is that you know. And I know you know because you brought it up to start with and I do trust your judgment." How the hell was I going to argue with that logic? As I was studying it out, he let go a round into the air and scared the shit out of me.

"Damnit Jack, I said put that thing away."

He laughed and said, "I just wanted to see if it still fired."

"Jack, I really don't know where Cubico is for sure. But you get me back to Key West in time to meet my island girl and we'll figure out where it is and sail there."

"You're waiting on your vessel to arrive before beginning the siege on Cubico, aren't you?"

"Jack, when it arrives, we'll sail her to the land of Cubico if it's the last thing I do." Jack seemed satisfied with that and he took the wheel, fired the engine and we made course for Sloppy Joe's.

I arrived to meet my island girl exactly where and when I said I would. She looked so pretty walking along, window-shopping her way to me in her own island time. She was wearing a long skirt that she had bought while Jack had us aground on that tiny island. It flowed around her swaying with her every step. It was natural cotton white with large burgundy and yellow flowers. Her tan flashed dark in the setting sun.

As she passed a gay bar, three transvestites came out wearing miniskirts and thigh boots. I overheard one say, "If she were a man, with that tan, I'd be all over that." The other two said, "Ummm-huh." My island girl smiled and kept walking towards me. The transvestites looked on as she wrapped her arms around me and gave me a kiss. One of them said, "What a waste." My island girl laughed and said, "Do you want one?"

Being my smart-assed self, I said, "One what?" The five of us had a good laugh and we bid a goodnight to the street vesties wishing them the best and I headed into Sloppy Joe's with my island girl.

There were no tables so we nudged ourselves in and ordered drinks at the bar. My island girl said, "You know, that black guy in the leopard mini was pretty."

I laughed and said, "I think I could have sweet talked her into anything, if he had been a she."

After a couple of drinks, we decided to walk around town and enjoy the night breezes and each other. As we walked, she asked how my afternoon of fishing went, I told her most of the story, and she had a good laugh and said it served me right. She was right, as usual. I had no excuse for starting the drinking at lunch except that I wanted to get the better of Jack. I guess this day ended a draw between Jack and me, I thought.

The night was perfect. It was warm, but not hot and every star twinkled. The moon was full and looked close enough to paint any color we chose and we could see the crater's shadows. We decided to go check the tide with the moon so big and close, I wanted to know how it would affect the ocean, besides, walks with my island girl were filled with electricity. Tomorrow we would check on my boat, tonight was for walks by the sea and making love.

The sea was calm and flat. We stuck our toes in, it was very warm, and that was it. We left our clothing on the beach. Hand in hand, we waded in, laughing like teenagers. "What if someone comes along and takes our clothes?" She asked.

"Too late to worry about that," I said. As warm as the sea was, her body felt even warmer as she wrapped her arms around my neck and cuddled close.

She whispered, "You know we could get caught?"

I didn't think deep nor far in search of a response. "This is Key West baby. We're expected to. We'd look suspicious if we didn't." That was all it took, she wrapped her legs around my waist, and I became hers to do with as she pleased. I whispered, "To hell with mermaids!"

She giggled softly then kissed me and said, "Are you sure you wouldn't like a mermaid?"

The moonlight had her eyes sparkling bright as any star in the night sky. I held her tight and our eyes met and locked, delving into each other's soul. The warm sea washed over our bodies and we could hear the other's heartbeats amplified by the night air and the sea. I knew no one on earth loved as deeply as we and knowing that made every moment special. We understood we belonged to each other more than to ourselves.

The tide had gone out without our noticing or caring until it was time to retrieve our clothes. We would now have to run the beach naked to our clothes and I was laughing telling her to go first. We jogged together to where we had disrobed and were still very wet trying to pull clothes on as they stuck to our salty skin. I yanked my shorts trying to pull them up and fell in the sand. My island girl did much better.

My butt was shining white as a winter moon with sand stuck to every inch of me and I tripped and done another sand roll while attempting to get up. Once I'd stopped laughing, I ran back to the sea and washed the sand off, then took my time getting dressed. "Let's get something to eat," I said.

"I'm starving." She said, "I can't go looking like this. Let's go to the room and let me straighten myself up a bit and then we'll go."

We strolled in the warm sand up the beach in the moonlight holding hands smiling at each other. It had been our first time to make love in the ocean and Key West was the perfect island for new adventures. By the time we made the street, we were almost dry. We stopped and I kissed her and tasted the salt on her lips. I wondered as we walked up Duval Street how anyone could be here and not make love in the ocean.

When we entered our room, she took me by the hand and led me into the shower clothes and all. We stripped in the shower and just held each other as the warn spray washed the salt from our bodies. The water felt good and I let it flow over me as I sponged her back with a body wash that smelled of strawberries. I couldn't wait until I could get her on our own boat all alone out in the Gulf Stream.

Later, we dressed and headed out on the town with intentions of having a good meal and turning in early so we could get an early start to the harbor and our boat. We had learned there is no bad place to dine on the island only that the characters everyone wants to be around favor some places over others. We were drawn to those places also. Like truckers at truck stops, long lines at restaurants symbolize the best food and atmosphere.

We stood in line at a little restaurant for an hour knowing it would be worth it. It was a small joint and reminded me of the home of a bootlegger back in the hills. The porch was a wrap-around and served as the gateway to heaven when it comes to seafood. The inside had not changed much from when it was someone's home. Each room had two to four tables affording an allusion of privacy and we were taken great care of by the waitress.

The walls were pasted with autographed pictures of famous customers seated at a table. I wondered if they had waited in line an hour to get in too. The photo that caught my attention was of Hemingway at the marina with two large marlin he'd brought in. It was signed, Best wishes, E.H." But it was too late for the marlin to wish anything. I figured, he was better off to have not lived to see today. Times had changed and the old man, I suspected, would be shunned for such an atrocity today.

That thought made me somewhat nervous because I was a throwback to the time when men hunted and fished to collect proof they were able to go one on one with anything and win. I didn't hunt over bait nor fish to release. Seven hundred pound Tiger sharks on three hundred pound test line were not for the weak of heart nor of mind. One mistake after hours of fighting, and it was over and you tie another bait and start over.

My island girl knew my love of the challenge, although I'm sure she didn't totally understand it. She had known me to sit in zero weather from before daylight until after dark hunting trophy whitetail and never see a single deer and the following morning do it again. Testing one's self against the elements, big game animals and giant game fish revealed the true depth of man's spirit and religion.

"Are you going to eat?" She asked.

I had been so deep in thought over the Hemingway picture that I had yet to take a bite. "I'm starving." I answered.

"What were you thinking about?" She asked, with a puzzled look.

"Oh, just about how this old world has changed since his time." I gestured toward the photo. "I'm not sure it has been for the better either. Things started to become real complicated about the time he left. Let's eat and go have some fun," I said.

The food was more than worth the wait. I had swordfish, oysters and crawfish with all the fixings. My island girl chose a shrimp and pasta dish and it looked very good. Afterwards, we had a drink at the Hog's Breath and a walk along the sea at Malory Square. I marveled at the big ships way out to sea and my island girl listened to me talk about where I thought they'd been.

She always listened to my stories and may have thought I was nuts. I always had a tall tale for ships we'd see. All ships came from exotic lands and the crews always had strange accents making it difficult to understand their English but pleasant to listen to, and I had an urge to go to their strange lands to experience adventures I had not even thought of. I talked of my dreams all the way back to our room and she laid her head against my shoulder and listened as I rambled.

After a sound night of sleep, we awoke excited to be getting our boat. We showered, dressed and headed to the marina. I saw our boat docked next to a smaller sailboat. The Island Girl was drawing a crowd. Her lines were long and sleek and as beautiful as any model that had walked a runway. Gawkers were gawking and talking. The captain I had hired to bring her down was talking with the Harbor Master. It seemed a serious conversation.

My island girl and I stood back and took it all in. Our lives were changing today and the change needed to soak into us slowly. We were gazing at or new home as she swayed, riding the small waves like the sleek vessel she was and showing off a bit for onlookers. Her masts were of oak, long and tall, standing taunt as one would expect from such a lady. We loved her at first sight and couldn't wait to get her out to sea.

I had never sailed but not having done something had never kept me from doing it. I loved the thought of the adventure. I wasn't dumb enough to think I could just sail her out on my own. I had hired the captain for a round trip. We would sail with him back to New York. He had assured me that by the time we made the harbor at New York, I would be a seasoned sailor. My island girl wasn't as confident, but she trusted in me.

We walked up and introduced ourselves to the captain and Harbormaster. We said our pleasantries then got down to business with our captain. I had leased a slot at the marina and I wanted to know it's location. The Harbormaster pointed to two sailboats down the third row and said, "The slot between them is yours." My boat may have been slightly larger than those near my slot but it was a good location from the looks of it.

"Who are my neighbor's?" I asked.

"Some singer to port and an old move star to starboard," he said. "We get all kinds down here. Never know for sure who they really are. Don't see them much. They're in and out at strange hours. Several like you, wanting to live a dream that never materializes. Here one summer and then gone without a trace." He was easy to size up. He didn't believe in dreams and that made him sour on the world.

I had no interest in feeding into his paranoia of folks willing to chance really living. All I wanted was to sail and get the hang of what I needed to know to do so. I asked the captain if we needed to load up on diesel.

"He said, in a staunch British accent that he had already filled the tanks with petro and once we had restocked the galley, we could make sail. "Well be out a week, make provisions and we sail." My island girl and I were ready and then some.

My island girl asked what I thought the captain was like. I told her I was a little disappointed in him as captains go.

She asked, "Why?"

I said, "Well, he didn't have a patch over one eye, a peg leg, parrot on his shoulder or a hook for a hand."

She said, "I can't believe you would hire such a man!"

I confessed to my sin and said, "I hired him on reputation only. I should have asked for a photo and I'd of known better."

About then, Captain Jack showed up saying, "I want to check out The Island Girl for myself. I've already surmised you've a turd of a captain, there mate." The captain looked from me to Jack and back to me searching for an answer he didn't find. Jack looked at him and then to me and said, "He must be English, by that I mean British. America does not breed such snobs and most snobs like this candy ass certainly veer wide of Key West. I think because they fear having fun. The English are a queer bunch as sailors go. Just look at how he dresses. He looks like a crew boy from that old TV show!"

I didn't know what to say, so I introduced Captain Jack to my captain who looked him up and down and said in a British accent, "What a bum. Such heathens should have never been let out of Botany Bay!" Jack did look a little rough as he scratched his chin whiskers. He did need a shave and reeked of stale booze as he stood there wearing only a pair of shorts.

After a moment jack said," Fuckin' limey." Then turned to me and said, "How much of this shit you going to take before I whip his ass?"

Jack was right; I didn't like the guy and I had no intentions of sailing from Key West to New York with him. But I had a contract. I knew we both must agree to break the contract or he received payment in full or he would have to return the down payment, depending on who broke the contract. I had to make this a unanimous decision between the captain and myself. If I fired him, I would have to pay off the contract, and if he quit, he'd owe back what I'd paid up front.

I looked at my sweetie and winked, turned to the captains and said, "Jack, I like your company. You come help sail her back with me." I nodded to captain Brit England and said, "Can't beat that for a crew, can you?"

He said, "If you choose to haul trash from a colony of thieves and rapist on this vessel, I would like released from contract."

I said, "Okay," and ripped my copy of the contract in half. He did the same with his copy.

Before walking away, captain Britt England asked,"What is it with that bloat?"

I didn't need to think, I just blurted out, "He's Captain Jack Sparrow and Rooster Cogburn all rolled into one. He's Dennis Hopper in 'Easy Rider'. He is Captain America and you, you stuff shirt shit, you and your kind never did and never will get it. He is Robin Hood and he's everything you British never could figure out how to whip! He is an American original. And Jack is right, you are a fucking Limey."

Captain Britt England turned to leave the dock and came face to face with Jack. He went to tip his cap to Jack and as he leaned forward to do so, Jack swung from the ground up catching Captain Britt England dead on the chin. His skinny knees buckled and just before he hit the deck, Jack nailed him again and blood spurted from above his right eye. "Damnit Jack," I yelled.

"What?" Jack said, as he jumped aboard The Island Girl and yelled, "Cast off mate! We're making sail the hell out of here!"

We followed him. What else were we to do? As we moved into the bay, I glanced back and that Limey was still down but flopping around in an attempt to get up. A crowd gathered around him as he tried to stand. Some ass in the crowd was pointing to The Island Girl.

"Jack, how the hell do you plan to get us out of this one?"

He laughed and said, "Did you see that Limey son of a bitch drop. I still got it! Do you have rum aboard? I could use a drink!"

"Let's get something straight here, Jack. It's my boat and when you pull shit like that, it puts me and my boat on the firing line. Hell, Jack, the Coast Guard may be alerted by now and coming after us."

Jack had a look as if he were reflecting on what he'd done. But then said," I asked if there was rum. I need a goddamn drink. Knocking a British turd out of that Limey made me thirsty. I sure nailed his ass good, huh? It's your boat mate, but never forget, I am the captain!"

I whirled on him and said, "You're the captain of your boat. I have not hired a new captain yet. Don't forget that!"

Jack fired back with, "Where is my rum. I'm an out of work thirsty captain. You wouldn't let a man parish from thirst, would you?" It was difficult to stay mad at Jack. I did envy his, 'I don't give a shit' attitude towards everything.' I liked him.

"Jack!" I yelled.

"Now what?" He said as if nothing had happened.

"I don't even know if I still have a boat slip to dock her now."

Jack said, "First rum, then we talk."

I figured he wasn't going to shut up until he had rum, so I disappeared inside the cabin to rummage for rum. After a long search, I concluded the Limey captain only drank scotch. I exited the cabin with a bottle of Johnny Walker Red, pitched the bottle to Jack. he caught it and without a word flung it as far as he could into the sea.

"That was it, Jack, and you pitched it into the goddamn ocean."

Jack never acted as if he'd heard my words. "Hoist sail and we'll make course for the Caymans, then Jamaica. Jamaica has the best rum and you'll know all about sailing by the time we reach Aruba."

My island girl came out of the cabin, shrugged her shoulders, and said, "We need supplies. We have nothing, not even our clothes on board."

Jack said, "I'll swing her around the island to a little cove. There we'll be well hidden and good."

Just the sound of the names of those places seemed erotic; Caymans, Jamaica and Aruba brought a big "wow" inside my head. I had dreamed this dream for many years, and now, with a true product of the sea and throwback to the days of free spirited pirates at the helm, we were living it. I smiled at my island girl and I could see it in her eyes she knew the same feeling.

"I said, "Get us to your cove and let's load up on supplies and see how she sails. It's not the best of times to ask such a question, but do you have a passport?"

He laughed and said, "Sure. In my shanty. But you'll need to go get it, cause they'll be looking for me after what I done to the Limey."

While my island girl was shopping, I took a cab to Jack's shanty, and that's what it was, a shack along a beautiful section of secluded beach. Then I went to our room gathered our belongings and checked out at the desk and when I returned to The Island Girl, my girl had already returned and we were ready to set sail for The Caymans.

The sun was setting as we tugged-up the triangles of white sheets of sail. They filled, sounding like a rug being shaken off the back porch as we slowly began cutting the ripples of small waves and gaining speed quickly. My island girl stood at the bow holding to the railing looking as free as the gulls flying against the blue sky. Her tanned skin matched the beautiful hand-rubbed wood of The Island Girl. I loved seeing her being so happy.

I watched the sails while feeling the motion of The Island Girl rolling over the sea. It was relaxing. Jack was telling me how we would tack, increasing our nautical speed getting us into open waters where we should find the same trade winds as Columbus and Blackbeard. I was only half listening because I had waited for this day a long time and I was going to savor every moment of this new life.

Darkness fell slowly as we made our way westward. My sweetie had moved to the galley and the scent of food drifted from the cabin and my belly was loving the idea of our first meal on The Island Girl. I had thought about how great this life would be and throughout all my scenarios played out over the years, it was never this grand nor special.

When dark came and the cabin and running lights reflected off The Island Girl against the blackest dark imaginable, I felt very small. The sails were ghost and we were alone on a sea very different at night. You could hear the water but even when looking over the railing, you couldn't see anything except blackness. All was silent except for the bow cutting a trail and somewhere very large fish jumping now and then.

With the call of, "Dinner's ready," Jack and I made our way to the galley and took seats at the table. A feast decorated the table as we admired it and complemented the chef; we drank a toast to The Island Girl and to adventures yet to come. I was not amazed with the meal, because my island girl knew how to do it up and she had really done so tonight. Jack showed he had manners and his behavior rivaled that of any yachtsmen as we ate.

The Island Girl navigated on autopilot as we ate. Jack had said that we were far from any reefs and still miles from shipping lanes and autopilot was safe and that if anything did arise, there was an alarm we couldn't miss. I took his word for it and my island girl didn't seem concerned. The Island Girl rocked gently on smooth seas as we feasted. She creaked a little when she swayed breaking the soft silence of the night as I refilled our wine goblets. The talk was lightheartedly fun.

After dinner, Jack cleared the table then headed to the helm. I followed him to the helm, wanting to feel useful but knowing I wasn't and really, I just wanted to smell the sea air and get a feel for the freedom on open water. We were now doing, and going where we wanted at our own pace. My island girl soon joined me on the bridge and we sat on deck, arms around each other being pulled through the night by a natural flow of the sea's freedom.

Jack was watching the instruments. I could see the hands sweeping in circles on both screens. The radar was clear and the sonar blipped that silly ping I used to hear from the Seaview, on the Voyage to the Bottom of the Sea TV series. I asked Jack about the need for the ping and he turned the sound off. The night was now silent except for the rhythmic roll of the boat against the sea and breezes whipping at her sails.

My island girl and I had our evening coffee on deck and afterwards, she was chilling from the night air of the ocean, and we decided to call it a night. I said good night to Jack and he said, "I'll wake you at 0:400 hours."

I asked, "Why four in the morning?"

He said, "I need a bit of shuteye now and then. I'll sleep on deck when you come up so if a need arises, you can yell." We ducked below and into the cabin and made for the master birth with the big soft bed.

We opened portholes allowing a cross-breeze carrying the soft smells of the wide-open sea to wander through. We could hear the mesmerizing wash of waves to the hull; a peaceful calming rhythm that brought a slightest lift, then relaxing to settle to

rise and dip again; a perfect syncopation in soft notes of a musical sea. This night, The Island Girl, the sea, the lovers became one; all part of a magical love for the other.

We made love deep into the night, afterwards my island girl drifted into sound slumber, breathing easily and looking content. I glanced at my watch and it was 3:30am. I closed my eyes to rest them a moment and the next sound was Jack yelling. I arose pulling on khaki shorts and slipping my feet into deck shoes. It took a moment to clear my mind and gain my sea legs, and then I headed to pull my shift.

Daylight but two or so hours away, I shook the cobwebs from my head knowing that I didn't know a thing about what I was expected to do, I took the helm as Jack settled into a padded lounge. His last words before snoring was "Hold the heading. I'll take her back with the sun." The only light was the running lights and the multi colored screen showing any weather and the course of other vessels and there were no other vessels.

There is no way to describe night on the sea other than once you've been there; you know what feeling alone in a big world really is. It doesn't matter how many are on the vessel, the aloneness is as solid a notion as the vast sheet of blackness before you. It is a time to earn and lose the trust and respect of others. Everything you do impacts everyone and all they do impacts you in some way.

Although I knew I wasn't alone, I couldn't shake the feeling. I could hear Jack snoring and knew my island girl was sleeping soundly below; I was the one facing night by myself. It wasn't a bad or a scary feeling, it was more calming than anything. When looking up, I was seeing the same stars as I saw from land, but it was different seeing them from far out at sea. And I wanted to show them all to her.

The Island Girl was actually steered by autopilot and I stood as a figurehead at the helm. There were alarms to sound if radar or sonar picked-up on another ship, shallow water or other obstacles in the water and icebergs were rare in the Caribbean. I was only an awake body to make all aboard feel safer. I didn't mind pulling my watch and was enjoying the pre dawn darkness surrounding me and listening to the silence and daydreaming about places we were headed.

Somewhere around dawn, my island girl brought coffee up from the galley and we watched the sunrise together. The smell of the sea and sipping fresh coffee as we sailed westward was surreal. There was no land in sight but gulls still circled cutting on the breeze and at times hovering before swooping to the surface for small fish. There was life everywhere out here and it was much like living in a painting.

The air wasn't cool but with the dampness of the sea it felt cool and we knew as the day deepened the heat would come. To port, we watched a pod of dolphins playing. They arched circling like a circus act and they came to check us out. They posed as my island girl snapped photos. We were in the moment and loving it. Farther out, flying fish leaped high above the surface seeming to have wings allowing them to defy gravity.

After coffee and sightseeing with my girl, I baited a hook with a large squid and tossed it out letting line trail out behind the boat. I also let a couple of teasers out hoping to draw attention of a giant marlin. I checked tension of the drag of my reel. I wanted enough for a good hook set but not so tight to break the line when I done so. We drank more coffee with our eyes glued to the trailing bait. Jack still lay snoring on the lounge. We had a good laugh at the awful racket he made.

He sounded like a small boat motor coughing, almost starting but sputtering-out only to do it all over again. "Jack, do you need your plug changed?" I yelled after we'd had all we could stand. He mumbled something and I said, "Rum all around. Wake up and smell the world." He rubbed his eyes and they looked as if they were not ready to give up the ghost. "I said, Hey Jack, get up and hit the shower."

My bait trailed a football field in length behind The Island Girl, the teasers about the same. The sea was calm and the squid cut a small wake on the surface as did the teasers. Any marlin or sailfish worth his salt would have no trouble locating them. I sat close enough to grab the rod if needed. My island girl had settled in towards the bow and was enjoying working on an already dark tan. I wanted to fight the big fish.

Jack came from the cabin looking better than when he'd disappeared into it. "I see you're back from the land of the dead."

He looked around and said, "Land of the dead what?" He had a clean-shaven face with the exception of a goatee and mustache, and a look of a new man. He still had no shirt and only wore baggy shorts. But he was clean and sober at the moment. "Are we near where the big marlin roam?" I asked.

Jack said, "Take a reading on the current. It'll tell you when we hit the Gulf Stream. When we hit the current, we're there. The big marlin hold to it as a feeding ground." His advice wasn't necessary, I heard the reel whine and it was bent in a half moon by the time I swung my head to look. I grabbed the pole and with all I had, set the hook hard as I could. It jumped slinging its head side to side and my god it was big.

Jack took one look and started hauling in the sheets slowing the boat's forward speed before I ran out of line. Once he'd dropped the sails, he headed to the helm, fired the engine, and put it in reverse. I was getting line back because we were going to the fish not because the fish was under control. That marlin was doing anything it wanted and I had no say in it.

"Close to a thousand pounder!" Jack yelled.

He arose from the sea in slow motion, arcing above the surface, bringing a huge heavy body completely free of the ocean. He turned, shaking his head, pointing his long bill my direction as he danced on air. His sword-like bill swished back and forth like Zorro carving his Z, as I held tight and prayed he'd stay on. His thick sides shook sprays of water like a wet Labrador fresh out of the pond. It was beautiful.

All the colors reflected in the sunlight like a million sequins as he quivered on air before dipping back into the sea and far from sight. He went down only far enough to make another run to the surface. This was his third jump and he showed no sign of surrender and showed only a fascination with challenging me in a battle to the death.

Jack yelled, "Keep him up. Don't allow him to sound."

But he was doing what he wanted.

I knew if he sounded, I didn't have enough line to reach bottom in more than a thousand feet of water. I also knew fish that size didn't get that big by being stupid. I held tight, but didn't try to do more. I hoped he would tire himself out. My only chance was to keep steady pressure and hope he didn't get mad before he tired. I was only thirty minutes into a battle that would take hours of testing my will against his.

I was where I had wanted to be for as long as I could recall. I had taken trophy whitetail, caught ten-pound bass and thirty-pound musky, but this was my dream. I was on my boat with the love of my life and we were living! We had taken a great chance to really live. I knew if it ended for me tomorrow, I had had a good time today, but I planned to sail the seas with my island girl for many years to come.

Jack kept the boat at a perfect angle with the marlin no matter where it ran. My biceps were feeling the burn and blue veins were standing like mountain ranges against the skin of my left forearm. The morning had heated up nicely and sweat dripped from my body pooling at my feet. This was the show I had waited a lifetime for and I never expected it to be easy. The honeymoon between the fish and me was ending.

This was now a war. Maybe it had always been a war, I just didn't know it. Some men were built for war and I was soon to learn if I was one of the warriors. I had never doubted my toughness but this battle could end quickly with one wrong decision. And that is where war gets tough. I have known many tough men that lost because of bad decisions. I did not intend to lose now or ever.

Being mentally tough is what won wars, being the meanest bastard means little in battle. The toughest, meanest and smartest bastard usually ended up the winner. All I had to do was outsmart a thousand pound fish. At first that had sounded easy. But this fish had no intentions of giving up and up until now, he had only toyed with me. He was taking line at a faster pace and Jack said, "Get ready. He's getting pissed."

Jack was giving moral support with words of wisdom. He said, "Fighting a big fish is like sex, about the time you think you got it, she'll throw you for a loop." I was half listening and thinking how hot the damned sun was. I said, "Hey, baby, mind grabbing me a cup of coffee? I'm a bit dry." Coffee was my spinach. I liked it with sweetener and a shot of milk. Everyone thought I was crazy for drinking coffee in the heat, but I did and liked it.

In my younger days, I worked a job where I pitched dirt with a shovel and it was hot hard work. An older gentleman working alongside me always wore long sleeve shirts and a denim jacket. I asked him one day why he wore all those clothes in the heat. His answer was, "It keeps a body cool to dress this way. A lot of folks don't grasp it, but it does just that." I guess coffee works somewhat the same with me.

My island girl brewed coffee and brought me a cup and I gulped it when the marlin was still. Jack yelled, "Keep his attention. Don't let him rest!" There was no real moving him, only holding pressure until the drag clicked. Jack had the boat right over him now and I attempted to get some line back. I pumped the rod and reeled down getting a few yards back. Then he showed he could take it all back and more.

I kept thinking, Jack was right, it is like sex and I knew this because I was willing to kill myself to prove I could get it done. I started laughing loudly. Jack and my island girl looked at me as if I had lost my mind. I said, "I'll tell you later baby. And Jack, you were right about this marlin fishing. What happens if he decides to sound?"

Jack scratched his chin and said, "I've been studying on that. I think I have a plan."

Jack went below and when he came up, he had a huge reel filled with heavy braded line and he tied a heavy stainless-steel split-ring to it. I admired his skill with knots as he twisted and tugged until he had it perfect. As he pulled the line, it snugged-up tightly and could not slip. "This is where it gets tricky," He said, as he slipped my line onto the same split-ring, then doing a little magic, he had attached the reel of braded line to my line.

He loosened my reel, let it drop to the deck, and attached the big reel to the rod as I held the big marlin at bay. Once the big reel was attached, I had enough line to hold him no matter what he chose to do. I was amazed at how calm Jack had been while making the switch. He had worked as if the biggest fish in the world was a bluegill. My island girl understood this was now more than a fish to me and to Jack.

I put more pressure on my fish expecting him to come up shaking that big head attempting to throw the hook but he held tight where he was. Then, he took drag and started down. Jack said, "Tighten the drag. Make him work harder if he's wanting to sound." I turned the drag three clicks and he was still going down. "Couple more clicks," Jack said, and I followed his instruction. Now was the time for patience.

I had read all the great stories of these big fish and the men that caught them. I had seen the pictures of the great fisherman looking confident, content and assured standing next to the giants hoisted by the tail. I wasn't feeling confident, content or assured at the moment. I wondered if they doubted themselves during the fight. I knew in my heart, this fish couldn't beat me by pure muscle. But I did fear making a mistake that would end the war.

"Want me to take him a bit?" Jack asked.

"Hell no." I said. "I'll win or lose on my own. This is a me against him fight until it's finished."

Jack shook his head and said, "It's just a goddamned fish, all it is, is a fish." I knew he was as wrong in saying that as he'd ever been about anything. This was not just a fish. It was what life is all about. It was about being tougher than anything and bringing the whole load.

I could feel him shuddering and fighting to take drag now. He was still going down, but I had him working much harder to do it now. It came with a price; the stress on my body had doubled with tightening the drag. There was now a large pool of sweat at my feet and I was hurting from top to bottom but I knew he was hurting too. Now, was the battle of will; of who wanted it more, which one of us was fiercer; of simple refuse to lose mentality?

All of a sudden, the reel began to squeal whining as though its guts were going to erupt. I was holding on for dear life. Jack dipped a bucket of water from the sea and poured over the reel. This fish was pissed and showing what he could do. If I tightened the drag another notch, I wasn't sure I could hold onto the rod. I had never felt such power. I could feel him through the line and he could feel me.

We were two boxers sparing checking out what the other had. I would need to be the counter puncher to win. I now knew I couldn't match his muscle pound for pound and he was more at home deep in the ocean than I was on the deck of The Island Girl. However it ended, a drink would have been the protocol following the battle, except, Jack had tossed the one bottle of scotch we had into the sea because it wasn't rum.

My arms and shoulders felt like I had just finished ten thousand pushups. I was weakening and the fish didn't care. I couldn't tell if he'd lost anything during the fight. He felt as strong as when we started this war. My mind wanted to meander and likely cost me the big fish if it did. I was hot and tired and my body wanted to quit the game but my determination to beat all of them held strong.

Jack had shut the engine down and as the marlin sounded, he pulled The Island Girl as he dove at a steep angle. Big fish can pull a boat for sure, but I thought doing so would take something out of him. The Island Girl wasn't a small vessel at eighty feet she drafted deep. "How long?" I asked.

"Two hours." Jack answered. "A long fight yet ahead if I know anything about Blue marlin." He said.

I was still game.

I could see in her look that my island girl was a little worried about me. I kept letting her know I was in better shape than the fish. I told her, "At least I don't have a hook in my mouth." That marlin stayed deep. I pumped the rod trying to get him to budge. He was content where he was and we had a Mexican stand-off going, or as Jack called it, "A Cubican stand-off." A shot of rum sure would be good, I though.

"Wait till we arrive in Cubico with this big fish. We'll be heroes. All true Cubicans will be buying us drinks. " Jack said.

What I wanted was a drink now, but Jack had ruined that possibility by just being Jack. I thought about what he'd said and asked, "What about the untrue Cubicans?"

Jack being Jack had it all figured out. He said, "We'll deport the skumbags and now we have the perfect method to know who they are."

Jack had a way of living for the moment and not giving a damn about the future. He just seemed to figure it would all work out for him. So far, it had. Three days ago, I had not even met him and now he was the skipper of The Island Girl. There wasn't really any big money in being the captain of this boat, but he seemed to despise those with money anyway, so he was in the right place captaining the right vessel. Life has a good way of bringing the right people together at the perfect time and I was in the right place and time and the fish was whipping my ass at this moment in it.

Just then, as my mind had moseyed off task for a moment, I felt something change in my fish and I returned to where I needed to be. He was no longer sounding. Maybe he was tiring, I thought. Jack noticed too. "Start cranking." He yelled! "Reel fast...fast as you can. He's coming up. It's an old trick. He thinks you're relaxed counting on him to keep sounding. He's wanting to put slack in the line and if he gets it, he'll sound again and the line will snap." I reeled fast as I could but couldn't keep up with him.

I couldn't keep up with the speed he was coming no matter how fast I reeled. He was moving fast to be that big and it boggled my mind he could do that. My arm could move no faster and the ache of the burn hurt badly. My body wanted to quit but my mind wouldn't let it. I wasn't about to allow a fish to tell me that I was not that tough. Right here, right now, is where and when, men can be broken forever, I thought.

I was feeling a pain that I could recall from having played football and tennis. It always arrived when you had reached a particular plateau and your body wants no more of what it is that it is being forced to do. I had fought this before and I knew I could win the fight with my body. I was still unsure about winning the battle with the fish. Every part of my body was saying quit but my hand and arm kept winding in line.

That fish kept coming. He was a bastard for sure and had all intentions of destroying who I was and when that thought crept into my head, I found a new reason to never let up on him. I was now intent on killing this monster before he killed me. We now had an understanding between man and fish. One of us was going to die to prove a point by the other. I knew I had the balls to finish the game. We would see about him.

Jack fired the engine and said he was going to pull away slowly in an effort to help get the slack out before the marlin decided to sound. I should have felt that I had an edge but it wasn't happening. As of now, the fish was holding his own, if not winning. I wanted to see him roll on his big side showing he was winded too. The time for giving quarter had passed long ago. We were sworn enemies in massive battle. One of us was going to leave this world a tired dead bastard today.

I knew if in the end, he could muster a final lunge, he'd put his spear through my chest and take me to the sea floor. I knew this because it is what I would do if I were him. I didn't hate him for it. How could I hate something that would kill itself to kill its enemy? That was a brand of honor no longer seen in men and this fish had it. It had a soul worthy of knowing. I was proud to engage him in such a battle.

I cursed at the big marlin and would have spat in the ocean, but I couldn't muster one my mouth was too dry and somehow kept reeling as the boat moved forward taking slack out of the line. Under my breath, I said, "So do you still think he's just a goddamn fish now?"

I said it louder than I'd thought because Jack answered, "He's a mean and smart son-of-a- bitch, but he's just a fish."

I knew Jack was wrong and Jack knew it too. He was attempting to assure me that it was only a fish and being only a fish, if I lost the battle it would be a lesser deal. I had been feeling him for hours and he was not just a fish. What he was, I didn't know. But he was not just a fish. He was something rare and worth my time. I didn't know too many people I would say that about. I loved fighting this bastard of a fish and wanted nothing more than to kill it. I wanted him to see me, to look into my eyes as I looked into his eyes. I wanted him to know I was the one.

All at once, the slack was gone. We were one with the other again. He turned to sound. But it was too late. He was tiring. I put my back into turning him. I felt his big head shake with the pressure I put to him. I was forcing a decision. He was going to have to take the pain of a hook in his jaw or turn and come toward The Island Girl. I wanted him to know the hurt too. I wanted to see if he was the tough bastard I wanted.

He swung that big thick head with jarring blows I felt through the line and rod, yanking my arms downward. His fight shook my entire body as if combinations from a heavyweight boxer were pounding me. He was one vicious son of a bitch. Every time I thought he was petering out, he rebounded with uncanny speed and power. He was letting me know I was not the master of the situation in any fashion. I was letting him know I was a bastard too.

He showed he wasn't ready to come to The Island Girl just yet by ripping off line. All I could do was hold the rod until the run tailed-off. I felt him slowing showing a small sign of tiring. I was not going to let him rest to regain strength. When he slowed, I pumped the rod and reeled hard getting small degrees of line each time. I could tell he was mine. The big power fight was in his past and I had him.

I yelled, Jack, "I have the bastard now." Jack killed the engine and walked back to observe the finish of the great fish.

But he couldn't do it with his mouth shut. "Bring him along-side, I'll gaff him." Jack didn't understand. This was my fight. I had no intentions of allowing Jack to gaff this fish. He deserved his end at my hand, no one else's. I wanted to bring him in, rope his tail and haul him aboard.

He began to come and I pumped and reeled and felt him slowly giving in to fate. He still shook his head and I felt it, but it was not the defiant hardness of before. It was as if he understood it was over and had given up. As he came closer, he looked huge and he was still a ways out and a few feet beneath the surface. His colors glistened from the sunlight. I could see his big dark eyes staring upward looking toward me.

I pumped the rod back and forth, reeling as I dropped the tip pulling him to me as I raised the rod tip and reeled. He was still cutting and tacking to make me work harder but he was spent. The fight was over except for when he would come close enough for the boat to spook him. Then he would make a last run or two. They would not be long runs but powerful ones draining the last of his strength. He had been a splendid adversary and in a way, I felt sorry for him.

It had been a wonderful battle. Many times during the war, I had not been sure if I would win. Jack glanced at his watch and said, "Four hours and thirty-six minutes and you still don't have him to the boat." I was worn thin, soaked in sweat and my body weaker than it had been in a long time. I was not going to allow Jack to get under my skin this close to the end. "Rig the boom, Jack." I wanted that fish to understand it was me on my vessel that beat him.

It had been me and him for over four hours in the middle of the ocean and now I had him. The closer he came to the boat, the bigger he looked. Jack studied him a moment and said, "He'll go twelve...maybe fifteen hundred pounds." Just as he saw the boat, he ripped off line and the drag sang loudly. He didn't go far, maybe a hundred yards before he slowed and I began to bring him back.

Jack had readied the boom and the big marlin was almost done. If he had one more run, I'd be surprised but he had surprised me before. I was taking nothing for granted. I could feel him quitting through feel of the line and I felt something deep inside for the fish that would fight so grand a battle being reduced to reeling in as if it were a log. He came along side The Island Girl easily and without struggle this time.

I gave my rod to my island girl and asked her just to keep a tight line. I could see she was scared. I told her it would be all right. As she held the rod, I grabbed the rope and made a loop, dropped it over and around the marlin's tail cinching it tightly. I held the slack out of the rope as I reached the switch on the boom and began to raise this giant fish from the sea. The Island Girl listed slightly with the weight of the marlin.

With its spear only inches above the deck of The Island Girl, I kneeled on one knee and looked it square in the eye. It was still alive but refused to acknowledge I existed, a last defiance of a great warrior. I saluted this big fish by tipping my hat and saying good words to the Great Fish Gods. I stayed at his side until there was no life in him. Such animals should never die alone lacking proper appreciation.

It was evening and I had not eaten all day. Jack suggested we take photos, get on with dressing the big fish, and have fresh marlin steaks for dinner. Eating him was the greatest honor I could bestow on him. It was time for the work to begin. I was tired, my island girl brought more coffee, and it tasted good. Jack was sliding a long knife along a diamond knife steel, putting a fine edge to it.

I stood triumphed beside the giant marlin as my island girl clicked photos. He loomed high over me making me look a runt. I had a smile but I also was sorry he had to die. Nevertheless, maybe it was better dying in a great battle than as an old worn out fish with only memories of what he had once been as his last thought. In some ways, he was a lucky to have died fighting while in his prime.

We worked hard to dress him and had a large amount of meat when we were finished. Jack knew his business with cleaning fish. There was almost no waste and Jack said we would use the innards and what other waste there was for chum to catch a few sharks for sport. The Island Girl had plenty of freezer space and we packaged and froze all but, what we were having for dinner.

The steaks were thick and smelled delicious sizzling on the grill. Jack and I could smell a sauce she was preparing and the garlic scent drifted from the steaks, swept aft on the wind and my belly wanted to get at the feast.

Jack said, "She knows her way around the galley by the smell of it." I thought about the fish and wondered, had it of won if the sharks would have found me as tasty as its steaks looked to be. I walked forward to get closer to the good smells. It had been a great day at sea, I thought as I watched the steaks sizzling on the grill.

We helped ourselves as soon as she said, "It's ready." I had never eaten marlin before and had no idea what to expect and was surprised by how tinder and flakey the big fish was. She had grilled the steaks to a perfect golden outside and the flavor of the marlin was outstanding. I ate in silence thinking of the wonderful battle. I thought it only right a man should fight to secure such a meal.

After we ate, I went below for a shower. Sweat of the day's toil had soaked me from head to toe, I needed rejuvenated, and the feel of warm fresh water and soap was the proper medicine. When I returned above, the sun was setting and a westward breeze forced us to tack to gain sail. I didn't mind the maneuvering, and a sober Jack was a skilled master, and I was gaining more trust in his abilities. I did love the sea.

Jack was an excellent skipper sober but maybe, I thought, the worst I've ever seen when drunk and he was drinking when I tagged him with the Captain Jack Sparrow moniker. It was difficult to hold a drunken partying spree against him; I've been told that I leave an easy trail to follow when drinking too. My island girl tolerated the two of us. I think she even got a kick from our antics and at times and Jack added a much-needed color to the English language.

We sat sipping coffee as a red sun reflected off white clouds turning the world reddish orange. My sweetie leaned her head on my shoulder as The Island Girl rode easily on the waves. Jack broke silence by saying, "We need to make land. I need to find rum and a woman. You don't mind another mate aboard, do you?"

I laughed and said, "Jack help yourself. Just pick a good one."

My island girl said," yeah, I could use company."

I was a little worried with what caliber of woman Jack would wrangle onboard The Island Girl. She was a big beautiful vessel and drew looks from most other boats and there was without doubt room for Jack to have a woman. I understood Jack's need of a companion. My sweetie was all for the idea. She could use female companionship aboard.

"How far to the nearest land, Jack?"

He was already looking at charts. "A day's sail to Little Cayman.

My island girl looked at me with a big smile and said, "Can I shop?"

Jack answered for me, "Cheapest prices anywhere are on Little Cayman."

I said, "It's settled. Jack, we could use a few bottles of wine, beer and rum. Think we'll find any of those on the island?"

He shot a look as if I were a loony and said, "Your words are pure music to these ears. Of course, I can find drink on the island.

Jack then looked at me and said, "Will you accompany me ashore?"

I looked to my island girl, turned to Jack, and said, "We're all going ashore."

"Good, good." He said. "We'll have a time of it."

I thought about what he'd said and followed with, "We'll stay as long as it takes. It's important you make the right choice in your woman. She may not be here at all."

Jack said, "Are you kidding me? They're all here and in every flavor too."

Jack was long overdue a rendezvous with a woman and I intended to rub salt deep into in the sore. "You know, Jack, you need to be careful in selecting the right woman. I hear many of them are on the islands only to find a girlfriend. A man may be swimming against a hard current if he's not real observant. I seen some real lookers on Duval Street and they were together, if you know what I mean! Just be mindful."

The seed was planted and I wanted it to meander, root and vine all inside him. I knew it would grate on him until he wouldn't know what to do by the time we made land. I was laughing out loud when I told my island girl what I'd done.

She said, "You're awful. Leave poor Jack alone."

I had no intentions of letting this go. Nevertheless, I kept my mouth shut to see what she would do. I knew she would attempt to help Jack in some way.

I wanted Jack to simmer a while. He was on edge and I knew his mind. He'd be worried about making the wrong choice and he knew if he did, I'd never let him live it down. He was right. If he screwed up, I'd be on him like sharks on chum. The sun was almost down and my island girl had a wrap to keep the chill of a sea night away. The sea was calm and I whispered an invitation to go below. I was feeling it after taking the big marlin.

Jack looked at me as she nodded a yes, and said, "You go to hell," as we disappeared below.

I laughed telling Jack, "Hold on there. You can make it one more night." I did feel a little bad for Jack. I had the greatest girl in the world and Jack, well, I was curious as to what he would come up with in a woman. I guess he was good looking enough and had a hell of a way about him. We'd see tomorrow how is luck runs.

I turned to my island girl and said, "I am the greatest marlin fisherman that ever lived."

She said, "If you had any sense, you'd have cut the line instead of almost killing yourself catching a fish."

I whirled and said, "Cut my line my ass. Didn't you see what I did today? I lived a thousand years in a few hours. Baby that was one of the greatest feelings in the world and I am one of the few to have ever done it."

"Come here and hold me with the same passion you have for catching big fish. I guess that's why I fell in love with you. You go at it full tilt never seeing life any other way." I followed her order and took her in my arms. She giggled and said, "I have you just where you had that fish, right where I want you." I had no argument. She had always had me right where she wanted me. I was a lucky bastard to have her.

Jack yelled, "Would you assholes keep it down? I'm blue balled enough."

She whispered, "What are we going to do?"

I laughed loudly yelling back to Jack, "Goddamnit Jack, you're going to ruin the mood."

She giggled and said, "We can be quieter I suppose?" I'd just caught a great fish and wanted to make love to my woman the way I wanted to make love and I didn't need to hear Jack's problems or feel a need to be quite.

After we made love, and I had rested a bit, I yelled, 'Thank you Jack."

He yelled back, "Fuck you!" I rolled over, kissed my island girl, and said, 'See, Jack's okay with a little noise."

She laughed and said, "Yes, I can tell. He's fine and dandy with it. And I'm the one going to have to face him in the morning. Being a female is not like being a man. Men brag and strut their asses in the mornings. It's different for women."

Now, I felt bad. She had a way of doing that to me. I didn't have an answer, so I said, "Guess we'll have to give up sex to make Jack happy."

She whirled saying, "I don't think so, buddy!"

I was over matched in this discussion. I had no idea what to say. I couldn't argue the point both ways like she could. I busted out in laughter and said, "We'll do it your way then."

Jack yelled. "Shut the fuck up."

The rest of the night was calm and I enjoyed listening the boat creaking as it shifted to the waves and breezes. Being rocked to sleep by the sea was not a bad way to dreamland and I loved my island girl cuddled close to me feeling her breathe as the smells of the salt air drifted across the night and through the berth as I relaxed listening to my girl as she slept. Tomorrow would be Jack's big day.

Jack woke me at 04:00 hrs to stand watch. I was sleepy but feeling the sea beneath the boat and knowing I held the fate of Jack and my island girl was enough to rid the cobwebs and help focus my eyes. The blackness of night on the sea was very much like being deep inside a well with only stars above. When I looked upward I knew the world was really big. Understanding how small we were made me keen edged.

Light came slowly but worth waiting on. The sky was first gray, and then the sun arose from beyond the horizon, coming up from the sea like the Phoenix. I was the only human to see this particular scene and I understood that. With the sun came the flying fish. They sparkled in the sunlight as they sprang from the sea to glide on air. This certainly was my morning to marvel at all that is perfect with life.

I wanted to wake her but somewhat loved seeing the act solo. I really didn't like the feeling of not having her by my side to see it too. In the end I decided to let her sleep. There would be many more mornings for us on the sea and she would be by my side for most of them. I eased below to start some coffee perking. I figured the smell of coffee would bring her around soon enough and I'd have it all then.

About the time I smelled coffee, I heard my island girl stirring below. Jack was snoring, still sounding more like a small outboard engine than human as I went below to grab a hot cup. I poured my girl a cup also and took it to her. She smiled, saying, "Thanks," and gave me a quick kiss, then saying, "I'm going to shower and then I'll be up." I headed on deck loving the day and this life.

Jack was snoring so loud that I almost missed the blip on the radar. I couldn't see it yet, but land was ahead, just over the horizon. "Hey Jack, wake up. Land ahead. Land Ho! Get your ass up and captain this boat." All that changed was his tone. Now he sounded like a stihl chainsaw idling. Little Cayman was almost in sight. For some reason I was looking forward to seeing land as an assurance the world was still there.

It wasn't that I missed land. I didn't. I think that I just needed to visit the sea from another angle so I could be in awe of it in all possible ways. Maybe it wasn't the land I needed to see at all. It may have been people. I needed to know they still existed and visiting land from time to time was an evasive way to see people. And my island girl loves shopping and I love her and shopping must be done on land and there I had it all figured out.

For all the good reasons, we were headed to land. This time, the main reason was so Jack could find a mate for a while. I never considered that Jack would want a woman for the long haul. He wasn't the type to be satisfied with anything long periods of time. I hoped he would stay with The Island Girl until I had a solid grasp of sailing techniques; or until I at least understood sailing well enough to keep us from dangerous situations.

"Jack. wake up! I need help navigating her in. Get up asshole! We're going down fast" That raised the dead.

He hit the deck running, yelling. "what...what...what we're sinking?"

I looked at how funny he was, hair jutting, looking like a crazed sailor wearing in an Einstein wig. I couldn't help myself, I yelled, "We're sinking!" just to watch the show. My island girl came running from below sacred and I had to call it off.

As Jack gathered his senses, Little Cayman came into view as an illusion, sitting low in the water; white breakers near the beach were spaced like yardage lines on a football field. It came out of nowhere, long and low with white sand reflecting wavy sunlight as a mirage appears in the desert. Green leaves of the rising palm trees at this distant, faded into the bluest sky with only a few small white puffy clouds drifting aimlessly about.

Jack said, "The easy way is to motor in, but you'll learn little about sailing like that."

I said, "Let's go in like the pirates two-hundred years ago did it." I watched the depth finder feeding info to Jack. I wanted to call out "Mark Twain." It just felt right to be thinking of him. I asked Jack, "You think we'll see Jimmy Buffett here?" Jack was all business while bringing The Island Girl into the harbor safely and he didn't answer.

Jack brought her in to where we could safely drop anchor. We hauled in the sheets and made ready to go ashore. Jack radioed to someone ashore for a dingy to come pick us up. He said that when possible it was easier to hitch a ride than to drop our dingy from its rigging. He said, "In vacation spots, they loved to taxi in the suckers, and if they want to believe we were suckers, why stop them?" I liked his thinking.

The shuttle took us to the dock and right up to The Hungry Iguana. I said, "Hell, I've read about this place in "A Salty Piece of Land."

My island girl said, "Let's eat and do some shopping."

Jack said, "You too go wherever you goddamn please, I'm going to have a drink then go on a scavenger hunt." We walked into The Hungry Iguana, Jack went to the bar, and we located a table and ordered food.

I heard Jack say, "Bring rum and keep it coming till I'm no longer here." He pitched a hundred dollar bill on the bar and said, "Well, where's the goddamned rum?"

I glanced at my island girl and said, "We'll be lucky to ever see Jack again. He's going to get drunk proposition a woman with no sense of humor and get his ass locked up, or deported."

She said, "Just let him run until he's winded. He'll be back." Then she said, "Where would they deport him to?"

I thought about it a moment and answered, "Cubico, where else?"

She asked, "Where is Cubico anyway?"

After I slowed my laughing and wiped the tears from my eyes, I said, "It's a fictional country to be invaded and named later. A long story, but Jack was drunk and I may have a few when we concocted the new nation of Cubico. But you'll be the Queen!"

"That's wonderful," she said. "Queen of a country that doesn't exist. Just how drunk were you guys?"

I said, "You really don't want to know, but we were lucky to make it back to Key West. All you need to know is you'll be Queen, I'll be the King and Jack wants to be Commodore or Admiral of the Royal Cubiacan navy. And he wants' to smoke Cubican cigars and drink a mixture of tequila and rum he's going to call it rumquila."

"I told you it was a long story. Jack loves the idea of having his own navy. I figured, what to hell go along with it and see where it goes. It made Jack happy and kept me out of a Havana slammer."

She looked at me sort of sideways and asked, "You and Jack went to Cuba?"

Quickly, I answered, Hell no. But we damn near did. Another long story you really don't want to know. Jack was just being Jack and yet we lived. Remember, I told you about it when we came back from that afternoon of not fishing?"

She smiled saying, "Let's eat, and then shop." The food at The Hungry Iguana was delicious afterward we had a drink and I checked on Jack before we hit the shopping trail. I reported to my sweetie that Jack was holding his own with the rum but like Rocky, would lose the fight and rum would be declared the champ by night's end.

It was a beautiful island and as we moved from shop to shop, I was happy with life. My island girl admired the tropical dresses and picked a couple to try on along with three new bikinis. After she had made her choices and we had purchased her new dresses and swimwear, I found a bait and tackle shop. She was a sweetie and went into the shop with me. I bought heavy braided line and a new heavy-duty deep-sea Penn reel. She took a deep breath when she heard the salesclerk spout the total. She had me now.

Last on the list was the few food items we needed. I hated grocery shopping so she let me off the hook. I headed back to see how Jack was faring. I walked back into The Hungry Iguana bar, Jack was sitting with a blonde on one side and a dark haired beauty on the other. He was thrilling them with tales of the sea and of his vessel. They were both in awe as he was spinning his web around them.

"How's it going?" I asked.

Jack answered, "Splendid."

I said, "I see. When do we sail?"

He said, "It's totally up to my lassies." He looked to them saying, "When shall we sail?" They appeared to be of substance and sober and sound of mind, with the exception of choosing Jack.

They looked at each other and the blonde said, "Let us gather our bags from our room and we can sail," as they left the bar to gather their luggage.

I stood there thinking about how this was going to be received. I had no idea how my island girl would react to Jack bringing two women aboard. I think she thought Jack was on a mission that was certain to fail and here he was with two pretty young women seemingly willing to be with him on our adventure.

Knowing Jack, I'm not surprised but I am somewhat amused at the mess he had managed to get himself into.

Jack's little scavenger hunt was sure to become one of the great mistakes of life. I could see no way that he could possibly survive the wrath he was about to induce upon himself.

I stood there shaking my head and Jack asked, "What's bothering you?"

I said, "Do you have any idea what the hell you're doing?"

He grinned and said, "Hell yeah, I'm going to be banging two sexy women and all three of us know it."

I said, "Jack, have you thought this through? Looked at every angle and see all that could go wrong?"

He downed another rum drink and said, "You must learn, my boy, to never dwell on the goddamned negative things in life. When the Gods of the sea hand you a tasty sandwich, you never question what's on it, you just start the feast. Feasts always end in due time. Worrying takes away from that time you have."

"Jack, My sweetie is easy going, but didn't you think you should run this past her first?

He ordered another drink, then said, 'She knew I was trolling for women, she had to have known there's no creel limit to how many I can catch. Funny ain't it? I caught two in less time than it took you on one fucking marlin. I short-lined them on fresh bait, for sure. Hot damn. This is bound to be an adventure a body could write a book about."

"Well, Jack, we're sure as shit getting ready to find out." There was no way this could end well. The only thing I didn't know was when and where it was going to blow. I couldn't help but grin and nod at Jack. He sure didn't give a damn about tomorrow as long as tonight was good. Maybe the whole world would be better off to have Jack's attitude. The other thing I knew is that it would not be a boring time on The Island Girl.

I told Jack to saddle up we were going to sail soon, then I left the bar and found my island girl sitting on a bench in front of the Hungry Iguana. She told me she had gotten the shuttle boat crew to load the bags into the boat and that they would be ready when we were. I told her we were waiting on Jack and then told her about his women. She laughed and accused me of making it up. "You'll see," I said.

While we were waiting for Jack's entourage to appear, we took a walk along the beach. The warm blue sea washed silently onto the whitest sand I've ever seen and as each small wave bubbled inward, sand crabs scurried to drill inverted tornados into the warm wet sand. I picked up my island girl and carried her into the sea, with her arms around me, it felt good and we laughed as we dipped between waves together.

We swam in our clothes bobbing in the soft surf. There was no doubt, we were in the world we were always meant to be. We were two overgrown teenagers having the time of their lives enjoying almost unnoticeable little things no one ever seems to take time to see. I felt a sand dollar under my foot and dived, digging in the sand until I had my girl that trophy. A hug and kiss was my reward. I was her pirate king and she my green-eyed queen.

We took our time savoring every moment before I carried her out of the warm sea. We were lying in the sand sun drying ourselves as Jack, and the girls arrived. I rolled over to my island girl lying at my side and said, "I told you Jack Shanghaied a pair"

She sat up, dusted dry sand from her arms, smiled at them and said, "Hello. Welcome to the crew of The Island Girl."

Jack said, "Let's make ready to ship out."

My island girl was at ease with Jack's shenanigans. He was the kind of man that once you had spent five minutes with; you knew he was the freest spirited man on earth. He didn't put on airs for no one and said what was on his mind. He was one that would walk up to a docked thirty-million-dollar yacht unzip and piss on it because it was there. Jack was Jack and was not going to be changed by anyone or anything.

I, in a way, admired Jack. He reminded me of myself to some extent when I was younger and before I met my island girl and settled down a bit. I reckoned that after considering it somewhat, life has a way of adjusting where you decide to pee. But, then, you always feel an urge. I hoped that Jack never lost his desire to piss where he pleased. He was a torchbearer for we that remembered way-back when.

One thing about it, all women seemed attracted to his less than giving a damn attitude and the two beauties he now had proved that. I knew they were in for a rude awakening if they thought they could tame him in the least, but two women with one Jack, it would seem that tame was not in their vocabulary. I only wondered how nuts it was going to get. On the upside, my island girl was cool with it.

The sun had set by the time we made The Island Girl and the western sky glowed rose-red making the world pink in its wake. Jack and I helped the girls aboard and he handed-up the bags. My island girl opened a bottle of wine and we toasted The Island Girl and her expanded crew until the night was black and Little Cayman lit-up in tropical neon and music traveled across the bay and we danced on deck to a live band playing on the beach.

We drank a couple of bottles of wine, mixed a batch of margaritas, and continued our little party. The island looked alive and glowing as sounds of talking and laughing drifted between songs. The band was playing everything from Buffett to Bob Marley. I held my island girl close as we danced to "Come

Monday." We were all feeling the effects of too many margaritas as the sea easily rocked us to the sexy musical rhythms.

Around midnight my island girl whispered, "Come below with me." She took my hand and I followed knowing too much booze always put her in the mood. She said, "Do you think Kim and Liza are hot?"

I had a buzz working and I knew there was no use lying. "Hell yes, they're about as hot as they come. That Jack is a lucky bastard."

She laughed and said, "He is at that. But you're not going to do so badly tonight yourself."

I loved how naughty she became when she'd been drinking and tonight she was in that mood. I opened the portholes and let the sounds of the island in. She lit candles and the dim flickering light highlighted every curve of her tan body. It was cool in the master berth with a good breeze that at times almost doused the candles before they flicked back to life. I ran my fingertips down her shoulders and she lay back.

We slept late the following morning. I awoke to the sun beaming through the porthole into my face and Jack yelling, I'm going to kick your ass. As I gathered my senses, there were other voices, all sounding pissed. I jumped up, pulling on a pair of shorts and headed to check out the commotion on deck. Jack was giving better than he was getting from the sound of it. I just stood back and listened for a while.

When I stepped out in view, there were two preppies in a small launch looking upward to the deck of the Island Girl screaming at jack. One yelled, "Hey, prick, who the fuck do you think you are kidnapping our girlfriends. We demand their safe return immediately or we will call the authorities and have your ass arrested." It was almost funny listening to their attempt at sounding tough. Jack seemed amused by them.

Jack grinned, looked at me and said, "We have a matched pair of queers threatening to storm The Island Girl and pillage our women. I think I shall keelhaul them both, cut their peckers off then run them through the gut with my cutlass before sending them to Davey Jones' locker."

The bigger one said, "We will not tolerate such threats from a simpleton such as you."

Jack said, "It is no threat, my friend."

By now, everyone was awake and scurrying on deck to see what was happening. Jack was on a roll and said to the girls, "Stand back or make ready to get bloody," then he looked back towards the launch and said, "Prepare to have your bags removed and hoisted with our colors you polecats. We'll use your balls for chum, your bags for wind gauges and your innards to grease the riggings." I shook my head grinning at Jack.

Jack grabbed up a machete we used to behead big fish, wielded it above his head, slicing air, let out blood curdling screams, and leaped overboard. He swam towards the launch, the machete between his teeth and you could see the fear on the young idiots faces as they stumbled to start the engine and get the hell out of Dodge. I could hear Jack's war whoop overtop the sound of the outboard, as they were full throttle going away. They never looked back.

Jack swam back to the Island Girl, I tossed a rope ladder over the side, and he climbed aboard. He was laughing as his feet hit the deck. He shook himself off and said, "I fixed them fuckers. They'll get a twitch every time they see a sailboat now." He turned to the girls and said, "Sorry you had to see that. But there are times it must be as so. Now, let's have breakfast, if you please. I do have an appetite."

I watched the skiff with the young men become smaller until it disappeared. The world was quite, except for Jack slinging profanity to the four winds. The Island Girl sat steady in a calm sea. Kim and Liza were slow to fill with life and seemed a bit hung-over. The drinking and frolicking all night hadn't slowed Jack the slightest. I headed to the galley and started coffee for the crew of The Island Girl.

My island girl asked how long we would be anchored. She was already in one of her new bikinis. She said, "If we're going to be here a while, I'm going for a swim."

I said, "Go ahead," and I went up, helped her down the ladder, and then tossed a raft to her. I knew she wanted to kickback on her raft and she knew I would bring her a cup of coffee when it was ready. She looked native dark against the blue water.

Kim and Liza were lying on beach towels on deck. I suspected still gathering their senses. Jack yelled to me, "How 'bout this? I got two women and between them, they cannot fix a man breakfast."

I laughed and said, "Jack, you're on your own. I'm not cooking you breakfast either."

Liza rolled over, sat up and said, "But Jack, what else do you want? You are so needy and we had no idea you were high maintenance!"

Jack gruffed something under his breath then headed to the galley. I could hear pans banging and Jack cursing and a few minutes later, he came up with the blinder pitcher filled with beer. He took a long gulp using both hands to hold the blinder to his lips, wiped his mouth on his forearm and said, "Beer, the goddamn breakfast of captains."

Liza said, "Jack be a dear and bring us some coffee and a couple of beers."

Jack wasn't fazed as he turned and disappeared into the galley. In a moment, he reappeared with two coffees and two beers on a tray. He had frosty mugs for the beer. He squatted, handed each girl a cup of coffee, stood up and opened the beers pouring them into the frosty mugs, and as the girls sipped the hot coffee, he took a mug in each hand and showed he was ambidextrous by pouring the beers over their heads in sync.

They were much more surprised than I. They were just getting to know Jack. He then announced, "I only recently saved your tan asses, and no question about it, I do like it that they are tan, from greedy land lubber gay pirates intending to take you by force from this ship and I suspect with intent to perform despicable acts to you and you show your ingratitude at my risking my life by not only not making breakfast, but ordering me, Captain of this vessel, to bring you drinks. I will not tolerate this treatment in the future. Now, ladies, would you join me for a swim before we weigh-anchor and set sail?"

The girls looked sheepishly at each other and said, "Okay." As they jumped up and each took one of Jack's hands as they walked aft and jumped in the sea. I stood thinking about what I had witnessed and could only shake my head in disbelief. My island girl was climbing back aboard and I took the tether-line from her hand and pulled the raft onto the boat. She said, "I smell beer."

I said, "No kidding."

We walked aft and looked off the stern at Jack and the girls playing in the sea. I said, "You would not believe what Jack just done and now he's swimming in the ocean with them. I don't get it, but Jack Sparrow, there, has the world by the ass."

My island girl said, 'It's that boyish wildness. No woman would marry him, but they sure like playing in his world. And they know it's only play."

"Well, I think he's a damned nut case and thinking about getting inside his mind is scary."

She laughed and said, "I didn't expect you would understand."

I said, "You expected right."

She hugged me and said, "Let's go below and make breakfast. Swimming has made me hungry." I wasn't that hungry, but I knew she liked breakfast. She took a shower to wash the salt off as I fried eggs and bacon and made toast.

I was just a coffee guy until mid-day or later but I didn't mind making coffee and fixing her breakfast. I went ahead and made enough for Jack and the girls to keep another Jack episode on hold for the time being. I think Jack hated when I stole his spotlight by cutting him off at the pass and I was beginning to think I was wrong about the girls and they may turn out to be all right after all and great company for my island girl.

I rang the boat's bell and yelled, "All aboard." Jack helped the girls up onto The Island Girl. They dried off and helped themselves to breakfast.

While they were eating, I said, "Jack let's sail."

He, with his mouth full said, "Arrrr."

I said."Arrrr?"

He swallowed and said, "Where should I set a course for?"

I winked at my island girl and said, "Set it for someplace we've never been. That's where we want to go."

It was a beautiful Caribbean morning of never ending sunshine, bright blue seas and a perfect breeze filling the sails as we hoisted the sheets. The Island Girl's bow bit into the water with the wind-filled sails. You could feel her move forward in a slight lunge as she came up riding smoothly across an almost flat sea. All three girls went to the bow like kids to watch the sea ahead. I nodded in approval of the scene.

The breeze caught the girl's colorful island wraps pressing the silk material against their bodies revealing their outline. The wind feathered through their hair and the view was reminiscent of a Sports Illustrated calendar shoot. I was a lucky man to be in such a place observing an extravagant amount of nature's beauty. I was surrounded on all sides by wondrous sights and living a life I never wanted to end.

Jack stood at the wheel whipping it swiftly by the large wooden knobs and as he spun the wheel, The Island Girl leaned, listing to the turn and he said, "We're headed for the isle of Martinique." Kim and Liza gasped, giggling like kids.

My island girl curled up in my arms and said, "We are really doing it. We are going to sail to all those exotic places."

I held her tightly, laughed and said, "Just like I promised."

The sea and sky were so bright both almost hurt your eyes, and the white of the sails made you squint like the sun. I knew little of Martinique, except it was an island and sounded exotic when my island girl said it. I was for it but knew we were passing many islands along the way. I figured Jack had some crazy ass reason for it being the destination, besides we were on island time so I really didn't care.

Once we made the turn, the Island Girl leveled-out and rode smoothly across the sea. Jack asked me to take the wheel and hold her steady. My island girl was at my side, we were riding high on our boat, the world was ours, and we were intent on enjoying playing with it for all it was worth. Jack had moved to the bow and was pointing out to sea, and had the girl's total attention with some tale I'm sure he was making up as he went.

My island girl said, "Look at that. He's living in a world all his own."

I grinned and said, "Reckon those girls know who they've hooked up with? Really, do you think they have a clue how nuts he really is?"

She giggled and said, "Those two can hold their own. He may throw them a curve or two, but they've been to town before."

I kind of grunted an un-huh, and said, "They haven't met a Jack Sparrow before."

Now, Jack had his left arm around Liza's shoulder as he pointed ahead then he waved his arm about and both girls were nodding in agreement, to whatever he was saying. As he wrapped-up that conversation, both kissed him on the cheek and he pushed Kim's hair back from her face, winked at Liza and headed back to where we were. I said, "I'm taking notes."

My island girl said, "You already have more than you can handle."

"Think so, huh?" I said.

"You're about to let your mouth overload your tail again." She answered.

"Yep, I don't know when to shut up."

She reached up scratching my head underneath my hat and I purred like a kitten. She laughed and said, "See, all the tomcat's gone. You're just a kitty cat."

I said, "Goddamnit, I can't help it if I like my head scratched."

"And your back. And your chest."

I said, "Alright. You win."

She said, "I always do."

I said, "I'll bet Jack don't have to put up with this?"

She said, "You may well be right, but Jack don't have what you have." I hated it when she was right and I knew what I had and so did she. I guess what gets me is; it would be alright if I knew, but damnit, she knows maybe better than I what I have. I knew she was the prize and that I was lucky to have found her first. But why did she have to know it too?

I had been looking at what Jack had, and couldn't for the life of me grasp it. They were well bred and from money. There was nothing cheap or unrefined about them, but yet, they took up with Jack, although it was easy to see Jack came from a very questionable background if not from under a rock. Most men dream of having a woman even close to the looks of those two and Jack had the both of them and didn't seem to care. Maybe that was it.

We were two hours from the last sight of land. The day was perfectly calm with only enough breezes to move us forward at an easy pace. The only ripples on the water were created by the bow of the Island Girl easing through it. You could look in any direction and the world we were in stretched only to the horizons with The Island Girl at its center. But at night, the world reached forever underneath an ocean of stars.

It was midday and I had the wheel as the smells of lunch drifted from the galley and lingered near my nose just long enough for me to curse hunger pains. Jack and the girls were below in their cabin and my island girl was creating the wonderful smelling lunch as I daydreamed of places I had yet to see. Occasionally, a dolphin or flying fish darted from the sea only to disappear again, leaving me to my thoughts.

When she said, "Come and get it," she knew I was at the wheel and couldn't come, so she brought up a tray for the two of us and she ate with me. It tasted as good as it had smelled and I took my time enjoying each bite of her swordfish and shrimp kabobs smothered in garlic butter along with tomato quarters, squash and mushrooms. She had brought the food of the Gods from her galley and I felt a very lucky man.

As we ate, the silence of the calm sea and full sails bowed easily to the west against the blue all around and was more a dream state than reality. But when she lay her head on my shoulder, I knew she was real and it was real and that we were actually doing it and it was better than I had ever thought it could be or had dreamed it would be. It was more an out of body experience than real and I had to shake myself back sometimes.

After lunch, Jack and the girls were still below and being silent. We laughed figuring that the night before had gotten the best of them. I said, "They've killed each other. I knew he was too damned old to party all night and be ready to sail all day."

My island girl said, "Those two would kill you because you're a lot like Jack, but that 'ol boy, he has a reputation to honor. He's not the type to die quietly."

I said, "And you think I am, huh?"

The next moment Jack was yelling, "A man needs nourishment if he's expected to perform all the duties as Captain on a voyage with two wonderful and loving women as you." About that time, he came into view and said, "I need a beer and some wine for the girls," as he pillaged a cooler on deck for refreshments. He tipped his hat toward us, took a swig from his beer, and disappeared back below. My island girl said, "You had better learn sailing fast. I've changed my mind and you are right, Jack is going to kill himself on those girls."

I shook my head and said, "Lucky bastard." She laughed placing her head back on my shoulder, as shadows cast by the sails were dark blue triangles to stern on the sea that grew longer by the moment. I leaned in kissing the top of her head. She sighed and then, we sat silently sharing the moment.

The next we saw Jack and the girls was at sunset. They came up from below swearing that they were starved. My island girl said, "Feel free to help yourselves. It's seafood wrap night. All the fixings are in the fridge and clean up behind yourselves too. I have plans other than cleaning up behind you three. I've raised my kids and you three are all grown up and haired over."

Jack winked at her and said, "Always a lady."

I said, "Jack, sweet talking again, are you?"

He said, "It's difficult to be me and not be sweet."

My island girl looked at him and said, "Jack, I am not spending my time on a meal for you and the girls. I know you don't think it, but the world does not revolve around you and what you want."

Jack touched his forefinger to his lips and said, "Keep that quite if you will. You are my queen, my lady." He looked to the girls and said, "Let's go below lasses. Cold food awaits our arrival."

We could hear clamoring from the galley as Jack made the best of the situation. "Girls," We heard him say, "Once you've tasted my shrimp and lobster wraps, you'll more understand heaven and I am certain after our frolic you will not be surprised that supplying heaven to you girls is my forte.

My island girl whispered, "He thinks highly of himself, don't you think?"

I whispered back, "I'm not sure he thinks much at all."

My island girl said, "Set the autopilot and come with me." She had the grill ready, steaks, and shrimp sizzling. "How…when did you do this?"

She said, "While you were gazing and daydreaming, I was planning a sunset dinner for us." I opened a bottle of wine and we sat watching the bow cut through a blue sea having a great meal and smiling at each other because we knew something the rest of the world had no clue about.

As we ate, I noticed a storm brewing to stern. Storms over the sea look more like a forest fire looks back home. The sky is gray and black from the sea upward into the sky as far as you can see is a solid mass. But, it was behind us and I knew I wasn't knowledgeable enough to guess it's direction. "Hey, Jack," I yelled. "Come take a look at this." My island girl said, "I think a storm is romantic."

I didn't want to scare her, but I knew storms out in the Caribbean is why there is a Mel Fisher museum. Ships have been disappearing out here for five hundred years and most have yet to be found. I grabbed a Jimmy Buffett CD and qued-up *You Can't Reason With Hurricane Season.* My island girl said, "You just have to challenge the Gods of the Sea, don't you." I said, "By-god, If you can't change it, challenge it."

Jack came on deck, took a gander skyward, gruffed something under his breath, and headed to the helm. He checked the radar, disengaged the autopilot and made a course correction. In a few minutes, we were sailing at a ninety-degree angle to the storm. I wanted to question the maneuver but Jack was a seaman and I trusted his experience with women and The Island Girl is a lady in every aspect.

The sea was getting a little choppy but nothing that raised eyebrows. The sails were full and the Island Girl seemed happy with the extra breeze and picked up several knots in speed with Jack's maneuvering. I looked at my island girl and winked as the wind blew through her hair. The temperature had dropped and you could feel the rain in the air. Jack yelled, "Batten her down for weather."

It only took a moment for the sea to change from choppy to six-foot swells and the Island Girl rode easily as Jack made another course change taking us dead into the storm and like my island girl, The Island Girl took adversity in stride. Jack had total control of the situation and was the calmest person aboard. My island girl had gone below to locate her Dramamine in hopes of avoiding the dreaded seasickness.

The rain had started to pelt us good. Jack said, "Go below, I have this." I was drenched and took him at his word. The Island Girl seesawed and was a carnival ride for me but my sweetie wasn't taking to it as well. She wasn't scared, just motion sick. It was going to be a long night if the Dramamine didn't kick-in soon. I felt bad for her because she didn't do well riding curvy, hilly, mountain roads back home and this was worse.

I could hear the wind-blown rain beating The Island Girl as we listed with the big gust and rode the waves high only to crash downward to rise again with the next swell. The sea thrashed us about for the better part of an hour before letting up to just a steady summer rainstorm. I heard Jack screaming into the night, "Not today. Maybe someday you salty-ass beauty, but you did not get me this day. I have seen you near your worst and survived. You sailor's whore, and killer of average men but you've yet to better me. I'll love you even as I sink into your depths to let you hold me forever you beautiful lovely sultry slut." He was screaming a dare into the night as rain drizzled his face and he didn't blink nor duck. He was a lucky kind of crazy. The kind of crazy you need on-hand and aboard.

Jack was as nuts as anyone I'd ever met, but he could sail a vessel half trying better than most men could sail giving it their full attention. I liked the son of a bitch more every day.

It wasn't that he saved our bacon that had me liking him, it was his go to hell spirit along with the boyish way he looked upon the earth seeing only a big round toy for him to play with and doing with it as he pleased and never worrying about tomorrow because he knew it would be okay. He loved living so much more than he feared dying and it was contagious to a degree. You either loved him or hated him. Or at times both.

As the sea calmed and the rain ceased, my island girl began to feel better. Jack was still cursing the night and the sea with a skill only a lover could muster. He was cursing as he entered the galley. We were laughing and he cursed us for it. I said, "Have a beer, Jack." He looked at me and said, "Fuck you and you two too," as he looked at the girls. He looked at my island girl and said, "Everything's okay now."

I went up to have a look, the moon was out, and the sky clear as if nothing had happened. If anything, the storm cleared the air making the stars and moon clearer and brighter than I'd ever seen them. The only thing more amazing than being on the sea at night was being on it during the day. And at that moment, I wanted it to be light so I could fish.

Every moment spent sailing was a spectacle in its own right. A dream is a dream but I thought living like this is a Hemingway novel and that one thought scared me. I headed back below to check on my island girl. She was sipping a soft drink and chatting with Kim and Liza as Jack was off changing into dry clothing. She smiled at me saying, "I'm over it now." I nodded and went back up on deck.

We had weathered the storm and I had a new respect for Jack. He sure could captain when the need arose. Most of the time he was thinking with his pecker and he always came close to letting his mouth overload his ass, but always seemed to walk away unscathed usually because the other poor assholes never seen it coming and sure never seen what hit them. And Jack was always somewhere else when they figured it out.

It took some time before I realized Jack had been serious that afternoon we headed out fishing and ended up drunk and heading to Havana. Jack was the real deal when it came to doing whatever struck him at the moment. I have no doubt, we would have been arrested in Cuban waters had we not ran aground on that little island. Drinking had an odd way of saving Jacks ass when it usually put most of us in deep shit.

Jack was a natural sailor and understood how to navigate on any type of water. He could look at the surface and know pretty close as to how many fathoms in was. He said the color gave it away. He told me if I would pay attention instead of goof-assing off I might be able to learn sailing too. In many ways, Jack loved to hate people. He always picked out their flaws and dwelled on them as if he were perfect.

The night now wonderful, a spectacular piece of work as the moon reached its zenith. My island girl had joined me on deck and we were star gazing seeing the occasional shooting star. Jack wondered by as a shooting star ripped across the sky. He pointed and said, "Them bastards are going to take over if we ever miss shooting one down." He had a beer in his right hand as he reached it toward the sky and shook his head.

I said, "Jack, what the hell are you talking about?" He pointed again and said, "Aliens. Those sneaky twisted little naked bastards have learned to ride shooting stars. It's a goddamned space rodeo up there and we bulldog them with lasers. They bust ass towards Earth and that tail you see is a direct hit burning their asses up. I'll bet when it hits them, their asshole's pucker factor is flat off the chart."

On that note, he turned and walked away. My girl said, "Do you believe that?"

I said, "No. And he don't either. He's seeing if we'll bite. He dangled bait and now he waits to see if he can get a nibble. The give-away was when he said they were naked. That would mean he's seen one."

She laughed and said, "He's a bad case of the whatevers."

I said, "You got to love his imagination? He's anything but predictable."

As we sat talking, another shooting star ripped across the sky. My sides were shook with laughter as I watched it burn in the atmosphere. My island girl asked, "What's so funny?" It took a moment before I could stop laughing enough to answer.

"I was imagining a little skinny naked twisted ass creature in a cowboy hat riding like Roster Cogburn, leather reins in his teeth, yelling "Play your hand, you son of a bitch."

She said, "Do you believe there is life out there?"

I said, "It's a big place. We know so little about it. But I'd like to know what's under us right now. Let your imagination go and picture all of the creatures below in the sea. Now double that with the oddest forms of life you can contrive. Those are the ones we don't know about yet. I think it smart to know what is here on earth before we rocket into the stars.

Jack came on deck with the girls and we sit talking on the subject of space and the depths of oceans. Jack said, 'There's things living down there that will never be found. There're way too deep and skittish." Liza said, "What do you think they are?"

Jack scratched his beard, winked at us and said, "Monsters. Killer monsters of the deep. The kind of monsters that's found only in the abyss, and in your nightmares."

Kim said, "Really?"

Jack had them. "There have been stories of ships pulled into the deep by sea monsters large enough to grab hold and crack the hulls of the largest ships, sucking all aboard to the bottom. The old time sailors and whalers tell of things to big and evil to harpoon. They say, the creatures roll to the surface, churning the sea into lather with waves big enough to toss men and wash them off the deck to their death.

In one ship's log, the captain wrote as he and his crew watched their sister ship being attacked said, "It was dusky and lamplight could be seen from the Haggin and night was closing fast. Then a giant rose from beneath the sea and all we could do was watch as it rocked the Haggin and we watched men going overboard. We could not sail to her for fear we would suffer the same. We could hear their screams and then the ship was gone. The sea calmed. There were no sounds and no debris. She was lost with all hands and cargo. We sat dead in the water until the following morning. That morning, at daybreak we searched and found no survivors and no sign the Haggin had ever existed. There were no bodies and not one piece of torn sail recovered. The crew is spooked and I ordered the 1st mate to set sail."

Jack said, "The ship sailed to port and every man including the captain left the ship to never sail again. They never talked about what they witnessed and the only clue to what happened was in the ship's log." The girls had scooted as close to Jack as they could get. Jack told the story in a spooky enough way that my island girl had moved close to me and she knew Jack was full of crap.

I couldn't resist assisting Jack. "Jack, do you suppose such sea monsters have survived and still live?"

Jack said, "This happened only a few years ago and not far from where we are tonight. That's why I thought of it. The keepers of written history always put it down to storms when a ship is lost at sea, but true sailors know. Very few first hand records survive to tell the true ending to many a poor soul being devoured by creatures of the deep."

Jack stood, grabbed a spotlight and said, "Did you hear that?"

Liza said, "Hear what?"

Jack flashed the light out into the dark water and caught a wave in the beam and said, "Whatever it is, it just rolled right there and churned the water." The way he said it rang true and the two girls had that deer in the headlight look.

Jack yelled, "Everyone to port and quite about it. They can feel movement and can locate you by sound waves."

"What is it?" Liza Asked.

Jack seemingly pondered the question a moment and said, "It is a wave. That's all. I just wanted to see if I could get you to port."

She wrapped her arms around his neck and said, "Jack, you're an ass."

Jack said, "I am at that, but a sweet lovable ass that has you wrapped around his neck." She shrugged her shoulders as Kim joined in giving Jack down the road over his behavior.

The girls all took a deep breath as we settled down into our seats. I had my island girl on my lap and Jack had Liza on one knee and Kim on the other. Both of them hand their arms around his neck and he looked like the cat with yellow feathers still hanging from its lips as he said, "Girls, why don't you make us a pitcher of margaritas and we'll continue our conversation about the bloody terrors on the open sea."

Jack was an ass, but not a bad egg. He was fun and much of the fun was in not knowing what the hell he was going to do next. I had observed that Jack had qualities the world could use more of. He read people better than a polygraph. He understood human nature. He knew what most people were going to do, before they knew themselves. That gave Jack an edge and he used it perfectly for personal entertainment.

My island girl leaned in and whispered, "Do you have to stay on deck tonight?"

I had no intentions of navigating anywhere but into her arms for the night. I said aloud so he could hear, "Jack and the girls laid around all day, by god they can stay up all night. What did you have in mind to do?"

She giggled and said, "I had you in mind to do."

I nodded saying, "I'm cheep, but I ain't free. You think you can afford a man like me?"

She said, "Honey, I bought you for next to nothing years ago."

"Yeah," I said, "But that was then, this is now and I've learned a few things since."

She said, "Okay, don't keep that education to yourself. Show me what you've learned."

I yelled, Jack, "You've got the helm till further notice. Try to get some rest. Leave those two girls alone. I'm fishing tomorrow and will need your help maneuvering The Island Girl."

She took my hand and led me down the steps, through the galley to the master suite. I was determined to play hard to get and doing quite well at it until she dimmed the lamp and pushed me back onto the bed. I knew she would rib me about this tomorrow, but I was smart enough to know when losing is better than winning. The boat slightly rocked with each small wave and the CD player on deck was playing Free Bird.

My island girl was my perfect partner. We had learned to get through the rough times by looking forward to these times and by understanding that we didn't do things to get under the other's skin on purpose, it was just a by-product of who we were. And right now, she was the world's greatest lover and my love for her was deeper than most could fathom, but that was all right with me.

I enjoyed that the world as a whole, didn't understand our relationship. I always got the impression the world thought I should give a damn about their concepts on living. I never understood why they thought my lifestyle was any of their concern and to be honest, I never dwelled on worrying about it more than this. I was too busy having fun living to give a shit about the rest of the world's uptight anal concepts.

We enjoyed each other and loved The Island Girl way of life. We didn't have a problem with Jack being Jack and somehow coaxing two beautiful women to join our adventure. The sea was our seven-course meal and Jack's shenanigans were the island spices that flavored every morsel. And Jack had an appetite for making the most simple thing or event an escapade into an incident and we never knew where they would end.

The one thing I was sure of, there's worse fates than being on a sailboat in the middle of the Caribbean late at night, making love to a special lady while listening to the sounds of Skynyrd as waves gurgle and roll against the hull. The smell of the open sea and the salt that crystallizes on skin no matter how many showers you take is intoxicating to lovers. I whispered, "I wished this forever."

She said, "Me too, baby."

The night air was damp and very warm. Sweat ran down my face dripping to the floor as I switched the fan on and headed to the galley for something cold to drink. My island girl said, "Bring something for me too, please." The humidity reminded me of summers back in Kentucky. The air back home was almost as hot and wet and some days when you breathed, it was more like drinking warm water a drop at a time than it was akin to breathing air.

As a kid back in the hills, summer nights were too hot for sleep. We had a window fan that circulated the moist air. I recall waking up soaked in sweat and kicking out from under the covers and for a moment, the fan made me feel cool and then it was hot again. But when I did sleep, dreams of fishing filled my head and I knew the next morning, I would dig a can of worms and head to Whaley's ponds.

I'd sneak out to the porch put an old straw hat on to cover my shaggy hair and keep the sun from cooking me. Barefooted and in a pair of cut-off jeans, I'd cross the highway, railroad tracks, and sneak to the ponds. They were pay lakes and I didn't have money so I had to slip in to fish always watching over my shoulder for the owner to come chase me off. The chance to fish always over-rode the fear of being caught. The only thing to ever catch me was my island girl. I smiled at that thought as I made drinks.

The Island Girl lightly swayed when puffs of wind caught the mains. I chipped ice, filled two glasses with iced tea, and made my way back towards my island girl. I recalled that as a kid, I never foreseen such places as we had already been much less where we were going. I smiled to myself at how far I had drifted from Kentucky. I knew I had worked hard and been a little lucky but I savored every moment anyway.

My island girl was partially hidden by shadows but I could see her silhouette as a sleek tan perfect shape upon the white sheets. She smiled and said, 'Thank you," as I reached the glass to her. I kissed her on the cheek as I slid in beside her and she felt so warm against my skin. She laughed as a cold drop of water dripped from the glass onto my stomach causing me to flinch and curse aloud.

We were lovers that were also friends and as happy as we had ever been in our lives. Her touch still gave me goose bumps and one smile from her in the morning could still make my day. Although, there's no way to be sure, but I feel that I still do the same for her. We were not cut from anywhere near the same bolt of cloth, I feel that that in itself made us perfect for each other.

As I was thinking all of this stuff, I cackled aloud thinking Jack is still cutting cloth like a mad man.

My island girl asked, "What's so funny?"

I told her and she said, "Poor Jack reminds me of you when we first met. You were just like him and you know it."

I couldn't find a good argument so I attempted to change the subject but she wouldn't let me. "Do you remember the afternoon we met?"

"Yes, I remember very well."

She snickered and said, "You were looking to do just what Jack is doing and you know it."

"Caught dead in the water." I said, "I was young with nothing else on my mind and to tell the truth, I haven't changed that damned much. I wanted you naked then and damn, I still want you naked. And lookie here, I've achieved my goal again you lucky lady you."

She said, "Yeah, but I got what I was after too."

We both felt we'd won the debate and that was good enough. We drank our iced tea and cuddled for the night to the rocking of The Island Girl as she eased through the sea. I fell asleep as she ran her fingers over my chest. She found humor in the fact I was like a puppy. She always said that all she needed to do was scratch my chest to get me to roll over and fetch. It felt good and was worth the occasional fetch.

This night was cooler but still hot. The breeze that occasionally drifted through portholes felt good and the fan moved the moist air about. Sometime during the night, it felt chilly against sweaty skin. I remember tugging the blanket up. The Island Girl was air-conditioned but I liked the thought of experiencing life on the sea as it could have been a century or more ago. In a way, I would have loved to see the Jolly Rogers appear on the horizon.

I awoke before dawn, staggered to the galley, and made coffee. I was quiet, not wanting to wake my island girl. I loved seeing her sleeping, rocked like a baby by waves. She looked so sweet and content and carefree. I poured my coffee and went on deck to watch the sunrise. The sky still grayish as the orange tint tipped the eastern horizon. I stood on the bow sipping coffee, looking back toward the east, smiling at it all.

I felt her arms wrap around me and she giggled saying, "I'm sneaky too." I was so caught-up in daydreaming that she had surprised me. We settled down and drank our coffee as the sky turned blue. She leaned over and kissed my cheek saying, "I love you."

I hugged her tightly kissing her forehead saying, "I love you too baby." We were living as free as any human could.

We watched in silence as the sun arose. The first rays were warm to the skin and I knew it was going to be a hot one. My island girl said she was going to make breakfast and disappeared below. I was feeling like fishing and the sea looked deep blue as flying fish leaped about. I thought shark fishing would be fun. I didn't want a long battle with a giant marlin this morning. I only felt the need to fish.

Jack made his first appearance of the morning rubbing sleep from his eyes complaining the girls were witches pretending to be wenches and their only intent was to wear his body into a weakened enough state that black magic and voodoo could wreck his health. He was drinking a beer and seemed in sound enough health to last a while longer and I told him to quit bitching about this life he had contrived.

Jack scratched his chin whiskers, gulped his beer and said, "Fuck them that's what I'm going do. They think they can kill Captain Jack by fucking him to death, I'll show them how I made Captain and it wasn't by ducking my duties. I'm going back to the grindstone and whit the saber to a fine edge. Yep, it's time to hone the cutlass and run them through."

I shook my head and said, 'Better have another beer, Jack!"

I pitched Jack a beer and he nodded and saluted as an officer going into battle might. "I'm proud to know you Jack," I yelled as he headed below. My island girl came from the galley with a breakfast fit for a king and was scolding Jack for picking food from the platter as he passed. "What's Jack griping about?" She asked.

"You wouldn't believe it if I told you," I said with a grin.

"Tell me anyway," she said.

I told her that he thought they were attempting to weaken him with sex to the point they could do him in by voodoo and that he was intent on being the better and he was headed off to the war.

She giggled saying, "Well, he took a hand full of fried oysters from your plate as we passed and was saying something about sticking something other than a pin in his little dolls."

I laughed and said, "He sure is game for the moment anyway."

She said, "Let's eat on deck." We settled at the table and with full sails casting triangular shadows to starboard, we ate oysters and quartered slices of fruit she'd purchased while on Little Cayman. Afterwards, I went below and brought up fresh coffee and the aroma of fresh coffee tangled with fresh sea air along with the view was intoxicating. We sat close without talking and enjoyed being together.

It's difficult to describe the feeling of knowing you are headed to lands where tribes of natives live much the same way their ancestors did when Mr. Christian took command the Bounty setting Bligh adrift. I had set my sights on seeing these places before I was too damned old to. I leaned back, my arm around my island girl knowing she was a little nervous too, but she always trusted me to keep her safe.

It seemed she had always been at my side on the quest for where I belonged, what I was supposed to be doing, and the answer to the silliness of life, she stuck with me and believed in me through it all as I searched. I think that we both knew that finally we had found where we belonged. It had been a thirty-five year marathon but by god we were now coming out the far side in decent shape and still deeply in love.

I leaned back closing my eyes and smiling to myself and the only sound was a few gulls yelping like hen turkeys and wind whipping the sails reminding me of old women back home shaking rugs off the front porch or shaking wrinkles out of bed sheets as they took them off the clothesline in the back yard. Man, I thought, that was a long time ago and certainly memories that were never going to fade.

Memories take you to the good and the bad. I miss some of back home but I'd never be happy with more than the occasional visit. I was too smitten with the sea and the Islands to be satisfied so far from them as Kentucky. The hills have a beauty that can't be taken away, but life among them isn't easy nor for the weak spirited. I owed them plenty and will visit them as a shrine but never again will they be home.

I opened my eyes, sat up straight, took my island girl by the hand and we walked aft to watch the dolphins follow in our wake. They come to check us out and seemed to smile to us. I smiled back to not piss them off. The sun heated the air, breezes begin to kick filling the sails, and we could feel the Island Girl ease forward as the bow cut deeper into the sea. This was the life.

Jack came up for air and looked like hell warmed over. I said, "Jack, it looks like the Voodoo is working. I don't think you can take another round of sticking pins in dolls." He grumbled while opening a beer. He drank as he rigged a rope tying one end around his waist and the other to a cleat and then jumped overboard. He used his arms to plane out and body surf. After a while, he motioned us to pull him back aboard.

"What the hell you doing, Jack?" I asked as he climbed back aboard The Island Girl.

"I was hoping a bull shark would bite my ass in half. I can't take anymore of those two witches. They're killing me and I won't stop. I needed a break and hoped death would take pity on me and save my soul from the hell I'm being forced to endure." He understood his role as a man and knew we were taking great pleasure in his misery.

I looked Jack in the eye and said, "How about some fishing?"

He smiled and said, "I have a yearning for yellowtail."

I broke out the light tackle to catch bait and Jack broke into the beer cooler. "Bring me one," I yelled. We sipped longnecks and slid shrimp on hooks casted out watching the shrimp sink deep. The wind lightened and as we slowly advanced toward a destination, we really didn't know.

My island girl and I were living as life is supposed to be. The sea was calm and could easily place one in a trance-like state. Knowing the sea is dangerous and looking upon these waters didn't coincide in my mind. Yet, a very intense part of any adventure was it must have some degree of danger, otherwise, it's just a boring non adventurous jaunt into the safety of entering a spook-house on Halloween as an adult.

Jack sat down beside me and said, "The ladies are taking a siesta. Let's hit the beer and ponder nature as only drunken sailors can." I thought, what the hell, I haven't been drunk since our trip where we started to Havana. I twisted the cap off another. Cold beer, calm blue seas, a sun getting hotter by the moment, an opportunity to set a hook on a hundred different kinds of fish and the woman I loved aboard is so cool, I thought.

I was on my third beer when Jack said, "Hoist the mains. It's time to see what she'll do."

I said, "Jack, we're having a great time. Why mess with it?"

He turned up his beer guzzled the last of it and tossed his dead soldier in a bucket and said, "Heat will bring the wind we need and I am going to ski behind this gorgeous bitch if she'll hump-up and do it."

I'd drank enough to say, "Why not?" I knew better but that damned Jack could make shit sound fun.

Jack tossed the ski overboard and he slid in behind it. I tossed the ski rope over as the vessel moved slowly forward. I was attempting to get this right in my head because I had never heard of anyone skiing behind a sailboat but that goddamn Jack was always up to shit I'd never seen before. He swam to the rope. I watched rope play out over the gunwale. Jack took the rope, gave thumbs up, and then put the ski on.

My island girl came topside just in time to watch the show. She asked, "What is he doing?"

I shook my head and said, "Skiing." The sails filled and we were picking up speed but I didn't think we were going to be able to bring him up. The rope played out then became taut. Jack grimaced under the torque but held the course and slowly rose from the sea. The son of a bitch was actually skiing behind a sailboat.

With not a cloud in sight, The Island Girl skidded like a flat rock across a still pond. The sea was slick as glass and smooth as my island girl's skin. The only action was Jack cutting a small wake fifty yards astern. Jack sure could ski and was gliding with ease. He was slowly drifting port to starboard to gain speed when I seen the swell behind him. Then I saw the long sharp bill break the surface and it was closing on him.

I waved and pointed to Jack. He gave the thumbs up. Before I could shake my head, the marlin hit, Jack upended, and it looked as if the sea had opened a sinkhole swallowing Jack and the ski. One second the sea was frothy with spray ten feet high, the next calm and smooth with no sign of Jack. I pitched a life vest as close to the spot as I could then turned The Island Girl back to search for Jack.

Just as I maneuvered the vessel close to the life vest, Jack popped to the surface. He took several deep breaths before bellowing out a string of curse words that would have made any sailor proud. The water around him was turning red and he was swimming towards the vest. He looked up and yelled, "That was one big fucker. Why didn't you warn me you asshole?" I dived in and swam out to assist him.

Jack yelled, "That son of a bitch speared me through the goddamn leg. " I swam to him and started working to assess the extent of the wound but Jack was all about cursing me. "You're sure as hell not much of a goddamn spotter. Here I am all chewed up and with two lovely ladies expecting my attention and affections this evening."

I said, "Jack you're full of shit. We need to get you aboard and see how bad you're hurt."

He refused my attempts to help him to the boat. Jack may bleed to death but he was one to bleed to death in style. He would die foolishly and for no good reason when his time came because he had to prove something that must be done all alone and before the eyes of the world. You had to admire him simply because he was Jack. I would bet even money he was going to bed the girls this evening just because he had already broached the topic setting the stage for another tale he would tell in every seaside bar.

Jack climbed aboard, hopping step to step on his good leg. As soon as he made deck, he was good. He didn't even limp once he was in view of the girls. Jack was a showman with the shit in his pants to back it up. He was a tough son-of-a-bitch any way you stacked it. Blood was gushing from the wound and he paid it no attention. He ordered a bottle of rum and a towel then took the helm as he thought Captain's should.

I may have owned The Island Girl but Jack was the bigger than life Captain of the vessel. The girls ran to him sobbing and he smiled and said, "Ladies, it's a tiny scratch." He sat at the helm, took a good pull from the bottle of rum, poured a healthy amount of rum on the wound and tied the towel around his calf. He said, "She'll heal fine. Ladies, I've been hurt worse falling from a barstool. Tonight we play."

Later that evening, chills set in on Jack and he was feeling the wrath of the marlin's bill. He wouldn't allow it to keep him down and the only way you could tell he was hurting was the drawn look on his face. I talked him into allowing the bandage changed. My island girl had a medical background and offered her expertise, I brought up the first aid kit, and she went to work as I stood-by wanting to see the damage.

The long bill of the marlin had pierced his left calf about dead center and gone completely through his leg. He had been skewered like a kabob ready for the grill. The tear in the meat of his calf was almost the size of my fist. When my island girl opened the wound, you could see how the muscle had separated and torn and it reminded me of slits made in deer hind-legs to hang them for skinning.

Jack looked down at the hole in his leg and said, "The bastard's got me pissed now. He was a wonderful fish. I looked him in the eye and could see he was surprised by what he'd caught. We're now brothers until death. I will kill him, I think." He squinted a bit when she pushed against the wound.

She said, "You're lucky, Jack. It's a clean wound and there's not much chance infection if you keep it cleaned." He laughed and said, "It was the rum. Rum cures all!"

It was late and only stars and the white of the Island Girl's sails flanked the night. The breeze was slight and silent as the sound of the bow slicing a fair sea was a barely audible sound as my island girl gave Jack a healthy dose of antibiotics and rewrapped his calf. Jack was feeling better and liked the idea he was going to keep his leg. But he now bitched about not getting the peg leg he said he'd always wanted.

The girls were Florence Nightingales, hovered over him and he was Jack. "Wench, fetch more rum before I die of thirst!" he yelled, followed by, "A man could starve aboard this vessel. Hey, you, the other wench, bring food before I become too weak to eat." They scurried after every order he yelled. I stood back with a grin. Jack never ceased to amaze me with his zeal for the dramatic.

He looked at me and said, "That goddamn fish took me deep before I pulled off. I thought my lungs would pop before I surfaced. That was almost too fucking close. And after all that shit, I don't even get a peg leg. The sea gods fucked me good on this one."

I was at odds with what to say. I took a breath and said, "Jack, sometimes it just don't go your way." It was difficult to know when he was serious or only acting.

One of the girls came with rum and a bottle of beer, the other, with a platter of oysters on the half-shell and grilled shrimp. Jack sucked an oyster from the shell, took a swig of rum and chased it with beer. "About goddamn time. I'm dying and all you wenches can do is think of yourselves. Fuck this, you are off this vessel when we next make port." They scurried off and Jack said, "That'll have them kissing my ass."

Jack finished eating in silence. I listened to wind in the sails and the sound of The Island Girl. My island girl brought up dinner and we ate on-deck without talk, both of us happily engrossed in the night. I wondered silently if Hemingway's "A Moveable Feast" was really about Paris in the 1920's or time spent at sea. There would be no answer found, except the one I chose for myself.

As the moon reached its apex, my island girl slid close, kissed me on the cheek, and said, "This is better than I had dreamed, except for Jack's injury."

I laughed and said, "You know Jack has kept the voyage from any chance of being dull. And if he don't kill himself, who knows what's next? "

She laughed and said, "But we aren't getting the alone time together I was hoping for." She had a point. Jack was a 24-7 project.

We were happy as could be living a special moment in time. We were cuddled and moving towards more. The night was warm with enough breezes to dry sweat but not enough to chill the body. Things were perfect and going great. Jack had gone below to the girls and the entire deck was ours. I said, "You want to?" She was all about it. It was our boat and we should be able to if we wanted.

We were alone; sure Jack was preoccupied with the girls. We had the entire deck to ourselves and were taking advantage of it when Jack yelled, "Cut that goddamn shit out and have a beer. I came up here, half crippled and with high fever to bring cold beer and spend time among friends to find you acting -- well -- acting like me."

I mumbled, "Bull shit!" Looked at my island girl and said, "I'm going to kill him!"

Jack laughed saying, "Ahhh, mate, but I may have just saved your ass from knocking her up."

I looked at Jack and said, "I don't see that a problem which we need saved.

Jack never being without words said, "Once at a seaside village on an isle off Trinidad, I met a seventy year old native wench that had just given birth to her thirty-fifth child. So be advised, I may well have just saved your scurvy looking ass.

With no words left after that line from Jack, I opened a beer and handed it to my island girl, and then took one for myself. To add insult to injury, Jack pulled the cork from a bottle of rum and made at toast that only Jack could. "To all the wonderful whores in the grandest of ports, even those too plain for the light of day but look ravishing before the light of the street when leaving the pub!"

Hell, who could not drink to such a toast? Jack had ruined my plans for the evening and he must have felt satisfied that he had accomplished some great good because he said, "Tis the wee hours and the girls await. I cannot linger and chance having them be sad." He nodded to us and limped his way across the deck and down below. My island girl said, 'Just hold me and tell me I do not look seventy years old."

I had to laugh; she looked so like a little girl that had just dropped her last piece of candy in the sand. As I held her, I could hear Jack yelling loudly to himself. "That pair of cocksuckers are the worst as drinking partners. You girls had better straighten your sorry asses up or prepare to ship the fuck out!" We sneaked-off and slipped into to bed allowing the sway of the sea to rock us as we made love.

I drifted into sleep and to that world where I thought Jack couldn't get, but in the back of my mind I knew it was a much more interesting world with him than it could ever be without him. Sometime during my dream, I longed for the day I would rule Cubico with my island girl and jack could navigate the Cubican navy to places never marked by charts and only existed in the minds of men such as Captain Jack.

I awoke early the following morning, eased out of bed, and left my island girl sleeping. I was all alone in the galley as I made coffee. The smell of fresh coffee filled the air as I started bacon and eggs for breakfast. I heard my island girl stir as the aroma of breakfast cooking made it to our birth. I poured her a cup and met her as she sat up in bed forcing the night away with a yawn.

I left her sipping coffee, went back to the galley, and made her breakfast in bed. She smiled and winked when I brought her breakfast, and asked me to return as soon as I could. I kissed her on the forehead and nodded. The morning was beginning to fill with sunshine and a nice breeze drifted through portholes. She turned the sheets back and I took the hint. It was a wonderful way to start-off a new day.

Everything was great in my life. We showered and went atop to meet the morning. On deck, Jack sat at the helm and it seemed the girls were taking good care of him. "Good Morning," I said.

Without taking eyes from his task, Jack answered, "It is a great fucking morning," as one of the girls fed him oysters from the shell as the other handed him a beer. He took a drink and said, "Yes, mate, a great fucking morning."

"How's the injured leg?" I asked.

He didn't answer my question as my island girl checked and changed the bandage. She looked at him and said, "You do know this will leave a large scar?"

Jack looked at her, then out to sea, as if pondering something very serious, and said, "You know it could have been a great white?" He stopped a moment as if in deep thought, then said, "Then I would have received my goddamn peg leg!"

I said, "If you're so damned set on a peg leg, Hell, I'm sure we can find a way to dismember you! You dip shit. The next island we make, I'll find the local voodoo witch doctor shaman son of a bitch and see if he will cut you friggin' leg off and your foul tongue out. I'm all about making you the happiest, most fucked-up crippled captain on the high seas." The girls giggled and Jack smiled at what I had said.

Jack laughed and said, "That's what I liked about you from the beginning, you're one to do anything for a friend. See girls, I told you it would only be a matter of time until he came around to sound thought. Now, by god, let us do some fishing. There's a large marlin out there with a taste for some of old Jack in his mouth." My island girl shrugged her shoulders and along with the girls moved forward to sunbathe.

As we made our way astern with the fishing tackle, Jack said, "The talk of the peg leg is all for the girls. When I made mention, they were in awe. I would as soon not, if you get my drift. However, wouldn't you agree, it would make an eerie thump while walking a deck late at night?" He smiled that Jack smile of his and he had that twinkle in his eyes that I was never sure of in relation as to its meaning.

We put a couple of teasers out, sat back sipping brews waiting. Marlin fishing is always a waiting game that in an instant becomes the most erratic, fast-paced moment in fishing until he's hooked and on. At times, hours of waiting for a few moments of excitement that can become quickly as hard of a life-sucking event an angler can suffer. Ahh, but the times he gets on and don't break-off can be better than sex to a true warrior fisherman.

Jack knocked back several beers and began telling stories of his trials at sea. "One time," he said, "in St. Croix, while visiting a local pub after several weeks at sea, I had tipped several steins of rum when this wooly gentleman I suspected to be of questionable ancestry. You see his accent was New Englandish and no seaman from the southern waters would ever ship-out with a half-assed American Limey... that talks funnier than a true fuckin' Englishman like the one I thrashed at the dock. Anyway, now that we have established his lack of proper upbringing and his pitiful drawl of the English language, I foresaw no reason to continue having him torture my soul with those awful sounds he mistook for a language, I tipped my stein to drain it. I didn't want to waste a drop, before I laid his head open with it.

I hit that asshole while he was in mid word and his knees wobbled like a landlubber's first time at sea. My stein exploded sending pewter fragments throughout the pub. He buckled, as all Limeys will when faced with the first bit of adversity. The barstool scooted like a creaky door easing open as he splattered to the floor. I was ready to make for the exit when the barkeep handed me a fresh stein filled with rum.

I looked to the barkeep. He said drink up mate and if he arises again, give him a second warning. About this time, his girl came in and attempted to get him from the floor. She asked what had happened and I told her he had had one stein a rum too many. She was not easy on the eyes anyway and any wench tolerating such a sorry sailor wasn't swabbing many decks, past nor future."

I said, "Is that it?"

"Hell no. That's just where things got good, mate! I guzzled my rum, turned from the bar to leave and they stood before me. Four of the most lovely of the wench species sizing me up for the kill. But, as you know, Ol' Jack does not make for an easy kill. I tipped my hat, never worried as to their intent. I smiled and bowed before them and took the arm of the two closest and continued onward to meet my demise."

He had my full attention with the story, maybe because I had had one too many myself, but I saw a bill breakwater, snapping at one of the teasers and I jumped up to reel them in and get the real bait out. Jack was readying the baited hook as I brought the teasers in. He made one swift cast and as usual, he was perfect and the baitfish landed where the Marlin had been. "I'll know him and he'll know me," Jack said.

With all the marlin in the sea, I thought, how could Jack think this was the one that had attacked him? I had learned a few things from Jack and one was; he had a keen sense of everything surrounding him. I was not going to question him right now. I knew if I did question it, and he turned out to be right, I'd never hear the end of it and it would end up being another story that Jack would tell.

I didn't like the idea that in something this far-fetched, he could still be right. I was reeling in the teasers as Jack readied a second bait and cast it out. Both baits skipped across the surface sending small wakes trailing behind. Jack stared out to the flat water as if willing the fish to strike. "Jack, what makes you think this is the same marlin?" I asked.

"I'll know and he will know," was all he said.

As the baitfish skipped on the surface, Jack tested the drag by pulling the line. Once satisfied, he placed the rod in its cup, grabbed another rod and let fly with another beautiful cast. All three baits were bouncing, skidding, skipping between the surface and a few inches below. "Jack wiped his face and said, "That'll get the fucker's attention," as the baits cut wakes in the sea. Now, began the waiting game.

I offered Jack another beer but he waved it off. I had never seen Jack turn a beer down. His stare was fixed on the flat water. He had one intention and that was to settle a score. I wasn't sure if it was because the marlin had maimed him or that it had, in his mind, cheated him out of a peg leg. With Jack, one never knew for sure. While I was in mid thought, the marlin exploded on one of the baits.

Jack eased the rod from the cup and reeled down until the rod tip was almost touching the water. With a loud guttural grunt, he whipped upward on the rod with all the strength he could muster. The rod tip bent down and the rod bowed. Every muscle in Jack's body tensed as the fish slammed upward from the sea throwing its head side to side and its bill slicing air so swiftly you could hear it.

Jack cursed under his breath as he struggled to hold the big marlin. It swished its big head as it slowly reentered the sea. No sooner than it disappeared, back it came. Its sides were silver and stripped purple. Multiple blues flashed strangely as the sun gleamed off his thick sides, throwing colors too pretty to be real from the fish. I thought only how wonderful the sea was.

The battle of wills was now in full swing as the marlin dove deep and the reel was singing as the fish took drag. Jack was holding his own by holding onto the rod as it bent almost double. He was leaning forward at the waist in an attempt to save his back and arms for the latter stages of battling. We both knew that because of the size of this fish, this was going to be a several hour war of the spirit.

Sometime during the early stages of the battle, my island girl began clicking photos of Jack and the marlin. I watched as she made her way to the best positions to get the shots she wanted and she did so without interfering with Jack and the fish and their war. She had turned photographing live events on the sea into art without getting in the way of the art. She was working every bit as hard as Jack was.

She squatted and twisted as the shutter clicked, then she would move again as the battle changed angles. Jack followed the marlin as it cut a rusty one way then the other. My island girl, like a cat, tracked the fight, creating a real time photo gallery of Jack's war. With the bandage hanging loosely around Jack's leg, he reminded me of The Red Badge of Courage with a slightly strange take. A true buccaneer, he was.

The marlin shifted direction and headed toward the bow. Jack followed keeping a tight line. It was spooling off line as if it wasn't hooked. All Jack could do was wait. Jack said, "Watch that bastard run. A fish such as that deserves me and no one else." About then the marlin leaped high into the air and bent in an arc, its big dark left-eye looked at The Island Girl, and it held hate in that eye

Jack yelled, "Turn you stubborn bastard. Show that portside eye! Show it, if you're the one-eyed bastard that dragged me into the sea! I'll tear out the good eye before we're finished!" There was nothing in the world to Jack, except the fish and himself. The sun bore down Jack and was covered with sweat. His wound was bleeding again. Blood ran down his calf, mixing with sweat, and covered the deck.

My island girl was in a world of her own also. She grasp the depth of the situation and there was no doubt that a chance to capture the raw battle as it unfolded would never be like this again. There was the fish doing what all fish do, fight for life and then there was Jack wanting to settle a score that could never be settled in any fashion other than in his mind. And there was blood being spilled.

Jacks feet were covered in his own sticky red blood. The bandage was loose and slipping down his leg and I could see the gaping hole through his calf. My island girl kept shooting as Jack kept cursing the fish. There was nothing other than victory and death for either. Jack was a scoundrel, but a scoundrel with more heart that anyone I'd ever known. Nothing held more meaning to him than killing this fish.

I glanced at my watch, it was reaching the two-hour mark, and neither had given an inch that they had not gotten back. The big fish rose from the sea again, shaking its head sending plumes of water skyward. It looked solid and filled with fight but Jack said, "It's close to death and it knows it's almost over." I didn't see it, but Jack must have somehow felt it. It just looked determined as ever to me.

Somewhere in my head, I heard the shutter clicking. It was nothing but sound that didn't really register as anything except confirmation of documentation to back a story that had yet to end. I was proud just be observing such a scene as it unfolded. Deep inside, I wondered if this was to be the feeling I would be chasing into the hereafter. I knew it was far too early to reach such a destination in life.

The marlin swung that big body in slow motion as it leaped and spun back into the sea. I noted that the dance of death was in full swing and somehow I was a part of it without being a part of it. Jack reeled down, and then raised the rod tip up bringing the fish closer. Now, when it leaped, only about a third of it came free of the water. It wasn't giving up, but it was giving out.

Jack yelled, "Fight you bastard. I'm not finished with you yet. I want you to feel the pain of the hook and to know it is me." Its sword came up swishing back and forth as if saying "No." Then it settled into the sea and came to the boat as Jack reeled. It rolled onto its side and slapped against the boat. Jack kept a tight line as he looked over at it snarling his upper lip. "Bastard," was all he said.

The big marlin lay still alongside as Jack stared into its eyes. "I told you it was the one," he said as he reached and grabbed its bill. He turned its head and the eye to its portside had almost been torn out. Jack said, "By god that caused it to rethink goring me." Then he just stood holding its bill and looking at it for several moments. Finally, he said, "You've met your match, you one eyed son of a bitch."

Blood from Jacks leg had begun a deep pool on deck and He had became aware that he was bleeding. He pulled the marlin's head up as far as he could, swung his leg over the side. He pulled its bill open "See. See what you did. You bastard." He showed the fish his leg, and then let the fresh blood drip from the wound into its mouth. He pulled his knife, the sun glistened off the blade, and he showed it to the fish.

He took hold of the line, yanked hard to make sure he had its full attention. "You taste that?" he said. Blood covered its bill and ran into its mouth and down its gullet. "You remember that taste. By god the next time you taste it, will be your last." He cut the line and the big marlin lay there as The Island Girl eased across the water leaving the marlin still on its side. Jack returned the knife to its sheath and said, "Bring me a goddamn beer."

I was exhausted, disappointed and thrilled all in the same moment. I had just witnessed the goddamndest fishing tale ever. Jack was Jack, whatever to hell that was. One thing I did know was that he could give lessons to world leaders on what being was all about. And he took it all in stride as it was part of everyday living and he knew no other way to be. That bastard was sure as hell different.

My island girl put her camera down and one of Jack's girls brought us cold beer. Jack sat in a chair and my island girl rebadged his leg. Jack looked up and said, "That son of a bitch thought he was dead as hell." He drank the beer, opened another, and said, "He knew I could have killed him. This is my Caribbean and now he knows I'm only letting him live in it. You see his goddamn eye? I ripped the shit out of it when he was sounding with me on his sword!"

Jack said, "I'm hungry. Can you wenches cook or are you letting the men starve on purpose? Grill some of that grouper we caught yesterday. Set a course for land. Let us make port in Cubico. I have a taste for Latino life deep in my soul. Let's do some nasty dancing." I winked at my island girl and she nodded that she was okay with making port. Pick your poison," I said.

Jack stroked his chin a moment and said, "Trinidad."

Jack's girls couldn't cook for shit, so my island girl took the helm at the grill. "How do you want it, Jack?" She asked. He didn't hem-haw saying, "Blackened, with Cajun rice and black beans." She looked to me and I nodded that I would eat too. "I think I'll fix drinks." I said, and headed below following my island girl to the galley.

She said, "Wow. Did you get all that with the fish?" I just shook my head in disbelief.

I made a pitcher of margaritas as my island girl seasoned the grouper. We headed on deck to the grill together. I followed her up the steps because I love looking at her backside and the mindset that women should walk three steps behind the man is pretty dumb thinking, if you want to see the beauty before you. I commented on her backside and she wiggled it and giggled. I smiled saying "Life is sure good."

She said, "All you men are the same, you don't love us for our minds."

I laughed and said, "Ahh, but I don't mind that you have one. I'll tell you when I don't like it. It's when you outsmart me. And you tend to do that most of the time."

She said, "It's easy to outsmart men. I know what you want and use it to my advantage."

I said, "I want to eat."

She said, 'Bet I can talk you out of it," about the time we made it to the grill.

I sat the pitcher on the table, turned the gas on, and fired the grill. My island girl went to work as Jack and I relaxed on deck and sipped margaritas. I poured one for my island girl and she gave me a kiss. 'I said, "It ain't going to work. I know what you're up to and I am not giving it up."

She just said, "Yes you will."

Jack said, "You need to take her below and knock the horns off her!"

She said, Jack whatever do you mean?"

With the conversation headed gutterward, the good smells coming from the grill brought directional change to the discussion. The grouper searing with pineapple slices and the scent of black beans and.rice filled the air as I poured another round of margaritas. The girls gave up tanning for the moment and scurried around the grill with mouths watering. Jack eyeballed them saying, "That Russian bastard would have been proud."

I cackled at his observation. He said, "What? That bell ringing Russian son of a bitch was onto something. Well, look at them? A man that smart probably was from the southernmost islands of Russia. Those igloo dwelling Siberian bastard-brains are frozen bags of chum. Most of them are queer, you know. And the rest, well, you've seen fat toothless Russian women? Is It time to eat yet?"

I said, "I hope so."

We dished-up plates and ate in silence. The girls catered to Jack while he acted like it hampered his style. My island girl could throw a hell of a meal together. Life on the Caribbean was hard to beat. There were a few sparse puffy clouds spaced out in the blue sky and the water as blue as the sky. The wave was action just enough to lightly rock the Island Girl and the sails puffed with the breeze as we ate.

After we ate, I went below to get charts. It was easy to pull them up on the panel, but I felt more like a true sailor doing it the old-fashioned way. Feeling the tools in your hand, measuring the distance on a map, and figuring time was more like real buccaneering. I loved looking at the islands on charts. It allowed my mind to wonder back to the day when cannon fire and looting treasure ships was the order of the day.

As cool as it would have been to have sailed with such men as Edward Teach or Henry Morgan, every moment must have been a fight for life. I'm sure there were good times but they were far and few between. Right now, I had it made. I was with the love of my life and we had Captain Jack, the most colorful Captain since old Blackbeard. I crack a grin every time I envision him whipping that limey's ass at the dock.

Ol' Jack jarred that asshole to his toes. What a way to find your Captain! I wanted to hit the son of a bitch myself, but he was a Captain too, and it seemed wrong at the time. But Jack didn't see it that way, he just cold-cocked him because he was a Limey and a stuff-shirted asshole. Jack had done what I had wanted to do. So, I hired him to Captain The Island Girl and I have only been sorry a time or two that I did.

We were Trinidad bound for music and dancing and hopefully great island food. I plotted a course and headed atop. As I made deck, Jack was bitching. "I should have cut its goddamned throat leaving it thrashing as shark bait. Look"? That bastard cost me dearly. One chance at a peg leg and that son of a bitch screwed me over."

"Now Jack," I said, "There's plenty of time left to get a woody to clonk around on."

Jack mumbled something beneath his breath and then said," He now knows Captain Jack and what I'm about. He'll not want a taste of Ol' Jack again."

I grinned and said, "Can't imagine anything wanting a taste of Ol' Jack, ever."

He hobbled off toward the aft and murmured a "fuck you" in my direction. He was doing all right. He had a beautiful girl on each arm and he wasn't as damaged as he put on.

What a day it had been and it was but half over. The sun was high, my island girl brought up another pitcher of margaritas, and we sat side by side marveling at the world at hand. We could hear Jack yelling orders at the girls but we chose to ignore him best we could. We were confident the girls were ignoring him too. I swept my hand toward the bow and said, "Somewhere over the horizon lays Trinidad. I wonder if it is really the island of the spices."

She leaned over, kissed me and said, "This is better than I'd dreamed it could be." I kissed her back and didn't say anything. The look on her face said it all and anything I had to say would have nullified perfectness. The air carried a light breeze with the fragrance of a fresh sea. I was more than satisfied to be here with her. I sipped my margarita and the sea salt on the rim of the glass had my thirst wanting more.

We sat holding the moment to ourselves and made it forever. The feel of the bow rising on the waves, settle in, only to rise again was akin to slowly making love. The slow wave ride was real and we were not missing a single moment of it. The sea was alive with motion. The sky was filled with life as birds cut and dove into the sea and we were the most alive we had ever been.

"What do you think Trinidad is like?" She asked.

I said, "Different, the smells of the island are a combination of sugary sweet tangy dark molasses mixed with strange and heavily spiced foods. The people dress in colorful garments much like what you see in African villages. What do you think it'll be like?" I asked.

She said, "I think it'll be filled with strange vibrations coming from odd looking musical instruments while people mill all about the markets selling goods, fresh vegetables and fish. The clubs will be all night events and filled with native music."

I said, "I do know that we'll embrace the culture and given the time, we'll surely go native."

She thought about it a while as if seeing a painting in her mind and then replied, "Yeah. I like going native. Let's do that." We were watching gulls dive on a school of baitfish. She would gasp when one folded its wings and drop straight into the sea. Sometimes they would reappear with a fish and sometimes not. Nevertheless, they were intent on doing damage.

We sat there an hour or more without a word just touching hands and being lazy. Somewhere along the way, I dozed off and when I awoke, Jack and the girls were finishing off the pitcher of warm margaritas. My island girl had disappeared from the deck. I asked Jack and the girls if they knew where she had gone. Jack said, "We were going to do nude sun bathing and she got up and left. Beats the hell out of me!"

I rubbed sleep from my eyes and said, "I don't blame her. Who'd want to see your white ass glowing in the sunshine?"

He said, "I wasn't going to do the nude sun bathing, the girls were. I was just going to observe the view."

I said, "Well, hell, that makes all the difference. I'm sure she wanted to hang around and look at naked girls."

He nodded, smiled and said, "Yeah."

I wished him the best and went in search of my island girl. As I headed below, I heard the shower running and decided to surprise her. I stripped out of my khaki shorts and eased into the shower with her. She was shampooing her hair and had her back to me as I slipped in. She jumped a little when I wrapped my arms around her but quickly rinsed her hair and settled leaning back into my arms.

This was what Caribbean afternoons were made for. The Island Girl was slicing through the sea on her way to Trinidad as we clung to each other as if there was never going to be another chance. We left a watery trail as we made our way, stumbling to the bed. I slipped on the wet floor and fell backwards, pulling her on top of me onto the bed as she laughed at me. You're going to kill yourself," she said.

I grinned and said, "You will save me."

She said, "I am the one killing you." The droplets of water falling from her hair felt cool on my skin as a small pool formed on the center of my chest. She said, "Look, a tiny ocean," as she created ripples with her fingers. "See the tiny waves," she said. I took a deep breath and said, "Tsunami," as the little pool ran off my chest pouring onto the sheets. Then we held on tightly.

Late afternoon was at hand when we returned to the deck. Jack and the girls were kicked-back beneath an evening sun still drinking. It was difficult to know if Jack was sober, a little drunk or plastered. His thinking and ability to conceive bizarre plans were a constant no matter his degree of alcohol consumption. I think one either loved him or hated him. There were no fence riders in Jacks world.

The thing about Jack was that he didn't care if he was loved by all or not. He wasn't going to waver to be liked. The world was laid-out as his toy and he was going to wear it out playing with it before he was finished. I don't think it was ever his intention to hurt anyone too bad, physically or otherwise, he had just set sail in a direction and was going with the breeze to his advantage and never spent thought on it.

He looked up at us and said, "Trinidad, huh? We're five days sail with this breeze and passing many an island with as good a selection as you'll find. Light skin, dark skin, nothing but skin and all have rum."

I said, "We'll stop on the return trip. I think we would like Trinidad and then other islands." Jack smiled and said, "Jamaica is to starboard and Cuba to port as we speak."

I knew where he was setting his heading with this line of conversation. I also knew that Jack would be willing to give it a try sober, and now that he was sauced, he'd go without another thought. With his luck, we would have dinner with Castro and be handed the key to Cuba. The thought was running around inside my head. I knew better but I had learned to trust in Jack's brand of luck.

It was good I was sober because deep inside I liked the idea of leading the Cubican nation. The king of Cubico did have a sweet ring to it and I wouldn't mind meeting and having dinner and a cigar with Castro. I had always liked Cuban food. Jack was just the one to pull it off without getting us life in a Cuban slammer. My island girl asked, "What are you thinking about so hard?"

I said, "You don't even want to know."

I must admit, I was taken with the idea of sailing into Havana harbor. There was the slightest of pirate in me. I wanted to break laws and see what our own country didn't want us to see. It was the same feeling I had as a kid that drove me to walk deep into the forests and climb to the top of the tallest hill so I could look over and ponder the view and then my soul always demanded I head to it. I had to see and touch it for myself.

As badly as I wanted to succumb to Jack's wild hair, I knew this was not the time. I walked forward, toward the bow to where Jack and the girls were. "Jack, I think we need to weigh all our options before sailing into Cuban waters." Jack stood a moment and then said, "You are right. Here we are thinking only of ourselves. We should be thinking of the ladies and what they may be forced to endure."

Something was wrong. Jack was gallant. He would never give in this easy unless he had something up his sleeve. This was on my mind as I nodded to him and headed back astern. I stood looking back at where we had been. It kept running through my head that Jack was way too easy in giving up on Cuba. It was only for the moment that I had Jack talked out of going to Cuba, and I knew it. It was not over by no means.

I stood in thought a little longer and then turned and announced it was almost dinnertime. Jack said, "Drinks first. They do seem to whet one's appetite so." Jack had been drinking all day. I grinned, thinking his appetite was about as whetted as appetites get.

My island girl asked, "What shall we have?" Jack said," surprise us as beauty always does. Create art for the pallet. The gullet will appreciate what it gets."

My island girl rolled her eyes Jack's way and disappeared below. I took Jack's advice and poured myself a rum and coke. I liked watching off the stern and headed back. Night was still a couple hours away but the sun was slowly losing its power and one could feel the night coming. It was a peaceful location to observe the world pass-by very slowly. A dolphin arced several yards out and then the sea was calm.

I glanced all four directions to the horizons. This world, to the eye was small and flat. I thought how alone one could feel out here. If it were not for having my island girl, I would go stir crazy wondering the vessel with only Jack as a companion. Jack was a wonder to converse with, but conversation and great fishing went only so far. Men without women would be a sorry bunch of slobs, but of course, Jack had two of them and I had one, so we were not short in that area in the least. I finished my drink and went forward.

I knew I was lucky to have my island girl by my side throughout this life. She was my anchor saving me from self-harm. Hell, without her, I'd be headed to Havana right now. All the luck was mine and I knew it. Not many sail the warm blue waters with the woman they have always loved and will love forever. Jack, on the other hand, was intent on loving as many women as he could. I had thought on it and couldn't see any way to really hold that against him.

As I awaited the dinner surprise, I recalled the days as a youngster in eastern Kentucky. I was around twelve when I first struck-out on my own into the green summer hills. I was unsure of everything except the feeling of how alone I was. I believe that men can only become confident men by testing themselves alone in the wild, whether it is the forest or out to sea, it is the testing that develops the man that comes forth.

I tested myself at an early age and came out of the hills knowing something many older men didn't. I waded in, too young to carry a gun so I carried a hunting knife. I had made sure the edge was a razor incase I was snake bitten. I was prepared to cut the X through each puncture and let the poison bleed out. The hills were full of copperheads and rattlers along with the tales of rabid skunks, foxes and raccoons.

Old men sat around on store porch benches telling of wild men with hair down their backs and long beards. They told of these wild men that came out of the woods foaming and frothing at the mouth. These stories were aimed at the boys standing around listening. There were stories of these men snatching up kids, running into the hills with them and the kids were never seen again. The old men telling the stories figured the kids had been eaten or worse. I wondered what could be worse!

Those old men knew I was at that age and it was only a matter of time until I decided to make my way into the hills, and they knew those stories scared the hell out of me. I can chuckle about it now, but it was real and true to us boys listening to them.

They didn't know it, or maybe they did, but they had done me a huge favor by forcing me to face the monsters and deem them inferior to me long before I was a man.

In my youth, I spent many days following game trails and climbing the peaks to get a reading on where I was in relationship to the rest of the world. I was never satisfied with just going deeper. There was always a hollow or tall point farther off that I had not scouted. I was at home being alone hunting for that snake I needed to kill before I rested. And here I was, much older now stalking a sea serpent.

I was rushed from my thoughts by the sound of my island girl whispering in my ear that dinner was ready. She rubbed my hair and said, "Welcome back." I smiled at her but couldn't get Cuba out of my head as I made way to the feast. She had prepared rice and red beans along with sweet scallops she had seared on the grill and corn on the cob she had buttered and grilled with the husk on.

The beer was ice cold and Jack's appetite now very whetted as he made way to the table. My island girl had set the table and the aroma of the different foods drifted slowly, an intro to what was to come. My mouth watered as I scooted up to my plate. I said, "Baby, this looks too good to eat, but it would be a shame to waste such a wonderful feast."

She said, "Thank you. It's nothing special." We both knew better.

I sliced into a scallop, popped a piece into my mouth. It was sweet, juicy and awoke every taste bud in my mouth. I salted the corn on the cob as butter dripped from my fingers, took one bite and it rolled my eyes back. I said, "This is fit for royalty."

Jack said, "If you please, allow me to rephrase that, It's too good for most royalty. Inbreads are too fucked-up in the head to grasp the greatness before them."

I laughed and said, "Leave it to Jack to drive a point home. Thanks Jack, You've made the meal a perfect success!"

He leaned back in his seat, his chest swelled and he said, "No, thank you. It was nothing really. I am gracious to have helped in some small way to make the evening special for everyone. Now if you will, I would love to offer a toast!"

I looked at my island girl and said, "Why not. Go for it, Jack."

He stood, holding his glass toward the stars and the toast began. "To the shellfish of which we cherish their meat. To the Indian for the maze. To the dumb fucking Irish and their potato. To the English for being gracious losers at everything. To the French who have surrendered their bread and country to everyone. To the limp noodle Italians. To all of you for being here on this magical voyage. I drink to you. Bottoms-up!"

With that, we finished dinner, my island girl left the girls to clear the table and we headed to the bow. The sun was half-over the horizon as we stood at the forward rail. We stole glances at each other. We both, I think, loved the look of amazement on the other's face. For us it was all about the other loving life. But we were always checking to make sure the love was growing deep, like the coming night.

As the big orange ball sank, the air grew cooler. My island girl began to chill, so I went for her a shawl. It wasn't cold, but night air had always gave her chills. I returned, wrapped the shawl around her shoulders and she leaned back in my arms as the sun disappeared and the moon arose. Stars popped out like fireflies as the darkness deepened. The lights of a jet at thirty-thousand feet flickered high above.

She looked at the plane's lights and said, "They're missing all of this. That must be an awful way to cross the Caribbean. We are so lucky." I kept silent and enjoyed the moment with her resting her head against my chest. I loved the sounds of the sea at night and the fact that the mention of sea serpents is much scarier at night. I smiled at my own evilness and held her tight while biting my tongue.

It was a full moon night. As it grew larger and higher, it highlighted waves creating never-ending silver chains of each wave. Somewhere out in the darkness a big fish splashed. She said, "What was that?"

I said, "Don't worry. It was a just a big fish, or maybe a whale. I hope it wasn't a giant octopus." She pushed tighter against me and I smiled and said, "It was only a fish leaping up to look at that big moon."

Even at night, the sea was filled with mystical sights and sounds, the Jetliner was over land by now, and its passengers had missed the entire point of living. Standing on deck, holding my island girl and with the largest window to the world, I couldn't imagine what a tiny look at the world they were seeing from thirty-thousand feet. Then, I thought, maybe there are people in the world that fear the opportunity of really living and they are the ones riding jets.

We stood snuggled, not saying a word for some time, enjoying the coolness of the wind in our faces. When she chilled, she cuddled closer and I done my best to keep her warm. We listened to the night and I knew in the back of her mind were thoughts of sea monsters. She knew that they most likely didn't exist, but there is always that chance of something out there that's never been seen by anyone that lived to tell.

I said, 'What's on your mind?"

She said, "I was just thinking about what's out there when we can't see."

I grinned and said, "Only what's out there when we can see.

She thought about it a moment and said, "That's not always true. Back home, there are the nocturnal creatures that are never seen in the daytime. Who's to say that the same isn't true out here?"

I didn't have a good answer, so I said, "You have me. And you know I won't let anything get you. If it's too big for me to handle, we have Jack, the dragon slayer. Give him a stage with a dragon to slay and he'd be in heaven!"

She said, "I'm not worried. I was only wondering about it." She was being a good sport, but I knew she was a little spooked after that big splash we had heard earlier.

Jack summoned me to the helm by yelling, "Get the fuck over here!" I heard the stress in his voice although he had tried to cover it with profanity. We headed his way. My island girl said good night to Jack, winked at me and went below. 'What is it," I said as I stepped to the wheel. He pointed at the radar screen and it looked as if a great green sky was ahead and in our path. 'What do you think?" I asked.

He said, "We need to get to fuck to somewhere else."

I looked at the screen again and said, "To where?"

He pointed out into the dark and said, "We should head toward Jamaica and see if we can maneuver around it."

I said, "Okay. But how do you know where it's going?"

Jack scratched his head and said, "Storms this goddamn big love land and the bigger the land the more they love it. Strange way they think, huh?"

Jack was on and feeling like talking. It didn't matter. He was going to enlighten me. I asked him our chances of avoiding the storm. He said, "Storms this fuckin' big are mean but slow. Slow as shit."

I said, "So we're going to out run it then?"

He squinted one eyes and said, "That's the goddamn plan, if it doesn't change its mind and decide to follow our course. Sometimes they like to attack helpless vessels too."

Jack was never satisfied leaving well enough alone. I asked, "What if it changes direction and comes after us?"

Jack laughed and said, "Ever been rained on from all four directions at the same time? This would be worse. If we get into it, it'll be sideways sheets of rain so hard it hurts the skin, all as we're being tossed in directions that don't even exist, as of yet. Sound like something, don't it?"

"Do we have another option?" I asked.

Jack said, "Well, yeah."

I said, "What is it!"

Jack said, 'We could steer to starboard, head for Mexico, but?"

I said, "But what?"

He said, "If we do and the storm stays out to sea, we'll stand to meet up with Mexican dope pirates."

I said, We don't have any dope!"

Jack said, "They are a sorry bunch. Shouldn't even be considered true pirates. Dope pirates give pirates a bad name."

"Here's an idea," I said. "Why don't we fire up the diesel and get the hell out of dodge?"

Jack whipped around and said, "No sailor worth his friggin' salt would stoop to being a motor boater."

I said, "But we're basically sitting dead in the water. There is no breeze and we're not moving."

Jack said, "We are going with the current, but, by god the sails will fill and we will sail. On that, I give my word."

I said, "Are you so against going to Mexico that you would risk our lives?"

Jack said, "The storm will go only one way. Mexican dope-heads are not so easy to plot. Dopers are reefs that move. They hunt. They kill. We have one storm and it's on the radar. We can track it. If we head to Mexico, we'll be on their radar. Besides, meeting one's maker in a great storm at sea allows the opportunity to become immortal."

I wasn't up for either, death was death, but there was no changing Jack's mind. I knew I had no choice but to trust him. He was a good seaman and he was the captain. What little I knew of sailing, I'd picked up from him. I had little choice except to hope he was right. I glanced up at the sails and nothing. The night was still with not a cloud in sight. Nothing but stillness with a sky filled with stars.

If I had not seen the storm on radar, I wouldn't believe it was out there. Maybe, it'll just go away with the night, I thought. On land, night weakens storms and they dissipate leaving a fresh smell to the air. Certainly, this will be the same, I thought. I figured Jack was making more of it than it was, as he is always the showman. I felt better about it now, and my thoughts turned to my island girl waiting below.

I bid Jack good night and headed below. I knew Jack would stay at the helm. Being Captain Jack demanded standing watch alone. Jack would have been insulted by an offer to stay and assist. Just being Jack, required suffering through and I knew Jack embellished such moments. It was what he lived for. I had never seen fear in his eyes. I don't think it had ever entered his mind that he could ever lose at anything.

I headed below and met the girls heading topside. That was more assurance he would be focused on other than saving our asses. I stopped by the galley and made drinks. As I entered our cabin and handed her her drink, she said, "Thank you. I was too lazy to move or I would have had drinks ready.

I said," You're welcome, baby."

She said, "Have you noticed how still the night is? It's a strange feeling calm tonight."

I said, "Don't be scared, but there's a storm brewing to the west and it's collecting all the breeze, I guess."

She sat up in the bed and said, "Is it going to hit us?"

I smiled and said, 'Don't get excited. Jack plotted a course around it. It'll throw us off a little on getting to Trinidad, that's all."

She got a thoughtful look about her and said, "If there's no breeze, how are we sailing around it?"

"A fair question," I said. "Jack has it figured out. He says the breeze will appear in plenty of time to sail safely out of its path."

She said, "Didn't we buy this boat because it had a motor?" You spent a fortune filling the tank with fuel. Shouldn't we use it if there is no wind?"

I said, 'To make a long story short, I asked Jack the same thing. He says we'll be fine that there is no need to use the engine."

She looked at me and said, "That Jack. He is refusing to give in, isn't he? That man would rather die as to eat crow."

I said, But he is very lucky and a good captain. Crazy, he may be, but he's a first class sailor. He may sound and act all rough and tough, but he knows the sea and he knows how to milk every drop of suspense from a situation and in the end walk away unscathed. I trust him to not get us killed."

She said, "You two are not good together. Jack is crazy and you're into his craziness. I love you to death, but you are as big a risk taker as Jack." My island girl had always allowed me a good length of rope. But she always reeled me in when she thought I'd reached the point where I was teetering on the edge. She knew when that time was, even when I didn't. She always had. Always, in hindsight, I loved her for it.

I knew she was referring to my length of rope when she said Jack and I were bad for each other. I didn't want to give up or in yet. I wasn't feeling any real danger but I knew my island girl was setting the parameters. The freedom to kill myself by uncontrollable urges of stupidity is something I had partially surrendered to this woman and I had learned to listen when that little voice tells me she's right.

There was no breath with the night air and the sea was flat with no pulse, not the smallest wave keeping the beat. Nothing moved and the quite was everywhere. The harder I listened, the more I knew we were in trouble. I had never experienced a hurricane, but I did recognize tornado conditions. I had seen this back in Kentucky just before all hell broke loose. It was time to bring Jack back to reality.

I sat upright in the bed, and said, "We got to get the hell out of here. There is no sense in risking everything waiting. Jack will just have to deal with losing his balls on this one." I had seen firsthand what a storm on Cave Run Lake could do to a houseboat. We were at the storm's mercy when it hit. It was a helpless feeling being tossed at will by wind and waves. I knew this was setting to end up much worse.

Jack was going to be pissed, but I wasn't interested in dying so he could play the part. I wasn't sure he really had the guts to do it, but I did believe he had the gall to not give in at the risk of belittling himself in anyone's eyes. Maybe he didn't give a shit what anyone else thought and it was an internal battle. Whatever it was, it wasn't a war I had the least desire to fight. I was here for the fun.

As I headed up toward the helm, I could hear Jack talking with the girls. Just as I made deck, Jack turned the key. The starter whirled and that diesel kicked. It thumped as it idled, sounding like an 18-wheeler at a truck stop. The dark filled with diesel fumes and shook with the vibration. Jack didn't know I was on deck as he turned to the girls and said, "I hope that cocksucker's happy!" I eased back below.

I couldn't wait for Jack to put his spin on it. I knew it would be my fault if we lived through a hurricane. I was snickering aloud as I entered our stateroom. My island girl said, "Well, that was easier than I thought it would be."

I said, "You have no idea." I lay back on the bed and could feel the diesel idling, sounding like everything was loose in it as the Island Girl eased from a standstill.

Jack slowly went throttle-up to about three-quarter speed. The Island Girl felt great under a good head of steam. The vessel seemed to glide easily through the water. I was happy to be moving. I was only hoping it wasn't too late to miss the storm. The sea and the night were both very calm and I felt better now that we were underway. I curled-up with my island girl and we nodded-off into the dream world together.

Sometime in the wee hours of morning, I awoke to the Island Girl riding waves and as she weaved, arcing lightly with the waves, I knew we had found the storm or more assuredly, it had found us. It wasn't bad yet, only a wave action we had not experienced and the newness caused concern in my mind because I had no idea how rough it may get. My island girl was sleeping soundly and I eased up, not wanting to wake her.

I made way to the helm. Jack was drinking a beer and watching the radar. I looked at the screen and it seemed we were on the outer edge of a brewing hurricane. I said, "Jack, how are we doing?"

He took a long pull from his beer and said, "I've been up all goddamn night alone while you've been frigging your brains out and snoring, that's how we are doing."

"So we are good to go," I said.

"Fuckin' ayyy," He answered.

I rubbed sleep from my eyes but headed back to bed anyway. Jack was wild but wasn't chasing a death wish so I knew we were likely in pretty good shape. We were doing all we could and whatever happens happens and losing sleep wasn't going to change a damned thing. I wished we had fired-up the engine sooner but that was a done deal and we were big boys and out to sea all on our own. Saving our asses was all up to us.

With the thought we were in great shape considering, I slipped beneath the sheets cuddling close to my island girl. She moved close to me as the vessel rolled in an easy motion atop the waves. I kissed the back of her neck and held her tightly as the boat rocked, swaying lightly, as if it were the swing on Granma's front porch. I dozed-off thinking how lucky we were at everything.

It was gray out when I awoke, the air warm but brisk as a good breeze blew through the portholes. My island girl was still sleeping as I pulled on my shorts and headed above. Jack was still there and still with a beer in his hand. He looked at me and said, "I told you the fucking storm would miss. Not being a sailor, you never have a fucking clue. None of you grass sniffing landlubber fucks ever fucking listen."

I ignored him and peeked at the radar screen. The storm seemed to have changed direction and was moving toward land. Maybe we had lucked-out. I hated it when Jack was right even when it saved our hides. He was a big enough ass anyway and everything he was right about seemed to add to that ego. I let out a deep breath and relaxed a bit. We were going to get wet but at least we were going to live.

Jack and I were alone on the bridge. The Island Girl was riding easily on the building seas when Jack said, "It's going to get rough. You do know, you're lucky as hell to have me?"

I glance in the direction of the wind. It was such a different ocean. The calm blue that was all around yesterday had been replaced with the steel gray of a bad winter day in Kentucky. I said, "I hope you're right about that."

It struck me as strange as I looked out across gray sky to the water how people fight over land and no one fights over ocean. Men fight on the ocean but never for it. The names of lost ships and rosters containing names of men aboard honor the brave never found. Just then, I understood the depth of night on the sea. There were so many ghosts held by the deep that night had no choice but be black and silent at sea.

Whitecaps lined in rows sweeping the gray sea east. The bow of The Island Girl took the waves in stride as she rode each swell pitching lightly between. We were a long way from Jamaica but far from the center of the storm. Jack had steered us well clear of the worst as the seas built with each wave. The Island Girl seemed small as I looked to the four winds and all I saw was swirling gray skies and angry seas.

Jack was still drinking and controlling the helm. The air was not cold but the cold blast of rain that came in sideways out of nowhere was. Jack yelled, 'She's a bitch, isn't she?" I looked and he was pointing out to starboard at a waterspout. It was cloud-white and the funnel looked perfectly balanced on the sea and reaching for the sky. It took a moment to realize it was not coming at us but going away.

Jack said, "Funny how spouts pop-up, isn't it? It is as if the Flying Dutchman wants our company, ay? " He laughed, nodding toward the spout and offered me a beer as he opened another for himself. I motioned I didn't want one and made my way below for coffee. As I measured the coffee, I was thinking how easily Jack took the world. He didn't take it at face value, but from the view that unknown forces were at work.

I started the coffee, peeked in on my island girl and headed back on deck. When I came into sight, Jack said, "She's sure as hell is a witch when she wants to be." I nodded. He said, "I was listening to chatter on the radio and the goddamned Mexicans are getting their asses thumped. I warned you about that. If it had not been for me, this vessel would be lying on her side on the bottom off the Mexican coast about now."

Jack was right but I chose to ignore him and instead stared out to the storm and horizon. The swells were growing but The Island Girl was sturdy and rode them well. It was not a good morning but it could have been much worse. The storm and The Island Girl were moving away from each other, my sweetie was sleeping through it all. I knew that was good because she had that tendency for seasickness in rough water.

As the morning continued along, Jack continued drinking. Later my island girl came on deck. Jack smiled and said, "Good morning, fair princes. I trust your slumber went well. Are my wenches up and about yet?"

She nodded, saying, "They seem a tad under the weather."

Jack said, "The drink and the frolicking are showing a weakness, I fear."

She laughed and said, "Jack, keeping up with you would wear on an anchor."

My girl was in good spirits and sipping a mug of coffee. Sitting down beside me, she asked, "Is the worst over?"

I leaned in kissing her on the forehead and said, "Yes. But never let Jack know that we know he saved our bacon."

She winked and said, "Okay." I put my arm around her shoulder, noticing she was chilling I pulled her close and held her tight as she lay her head on my shoulder.

Jack had spent the morning drinking and rearming the mast with sails. He hated the thought of diesel power. To Jack, using anything except the wind was thumbing your nose at the Great Gods of the Sea and he was having no part of that. I don't think he was as superstitious as he was a showman. He had no intentions of being upstaged by hurricanes, flashy women or pirates of a by-gone era.

We sat quietly listening to the wind baffled by the sails. They were full and bowed and The Island Girl slashed through the sea as if she owned every salty drop. Jack stood at the wheel steering a madman's course for Jamaica. He had switched from beer to rum because as he said, "No captain worth a sad sailor's piss drinks beer beyond noon with the exception of a beer for dinner." He offered me a slug and I waved it off so he poured a shot in my coffee.

I sipped my coffee the rum was strong. I shivered at it. Jack seen me shiver and said, 'It'll clean the ugly out of your ass. I give my word; you'll feel a better man for it." I took another sip and still shivered so I headed to the galley to get a fresh cup but decided to spice it up instead. A little sugar and cinnamon made it better. When I returned to the deck, Jack said, "You fucking' Shelia."

I shot a look his way and said, "Jack you have any idea who's picking up the tab for this?"

Jack said, "Yeah, and I must admit, you are a sorry ass role model. You go to bed before daylight. You drink sweet tea when there is rum aplenty. You make morning coffee for your lady and then tote it to her. The girls, at times, are observant and they may think this shit is normal or even worse, they may think it right."

I realized then there was no arguing with Jack. He lived by what at face value seemed complicated rules until you strip away all the crap and then he just lived as he pleased at a given moment and was not changing for anyone or anything. It meant nothing to him how the world perceived his lifestyle. Once you grasp the fact Jack was one of the few really free humans in the world, it was easier to let it slide but you never got totally used to it.

I walked to my island girl and took a seat beside her. She whispered, "Why don't you fire him?"

I didn't have to think about it as I said, "Jack is the kid in a candy store. He knows the store inside out and loves looking at the candy but never really deciding on one piece. He wants it all and that will never change. Sometimes, I think we should thank the Gods for our Jack. For him, life's no more than a whelm."

I looked toward Jack; he had one hand to the wheel while tipping a bottle of rum with the other. Southward, sunshine broke through bringing slashes of light from a center point, and then a rainbow appeared to the horizon. Jack pointed to it saying, "Goddamned leprechauns leach into a pirate's dreams to steal his treasures hauling them to the end of the fucking rainbows. They're sneaky little cocksuckers for sure."

I said, "Jack, my boy, they don't get you when you sleep. They get you when you pass out."

Jack raked the stubble on his chin and said, "Treasure's in the eye of the beholder and I've been anchored to a pair of black widow dolls intent on sucking the marrow from my soul far too long. Where's a goddamn Irish lep when you need him?" My island girl said, "who's up for a late breakfast? I'm heading to the galley. "

I said, "What's on the menu?"

She said, "What do you want?"

Jack popped off, "Steak and eggs with shrimp and fried conch fritters works for me."

She looked to me and I shrugged my shoulders saying, "Sounds good to me. Want any help?"

She said, "I have this one, besides, we don't want to put Jack in an awkward position with his spiders."

Jack took a pull of rum and said, "I knew you two would see it my way."

While my sweetie worked her magic in the galley, Jack explained how screwed-up people were. "You know, every morning there's millions of people going to work," he said. "They take cabs with drivers that speak every language but English or walk concrete sidewalks to the doors of buildings that blot the sun to offices with paintings of sailing ships and tropical islands on the walls and all for a week of vacation each year to where we live inside those painting."

Jack was right but it takes more than wanting to, to live here. If you are not born to it, you sell your soul for it. Everything you have known is left behind. It's not for everyone and you had better have made peace with the decision or it's no good. Some people must keep an iron in the fire and cannot look away from the flame never understanding it is not the flame, but what it lights beyond that's important.

As I was thinking on what Jack had said he popped off again, "It's a good thing for men like us that so many don't know when they have enough. The greedy bastards are never satisfied with enough. They want it all. I wouldn't swap places with 'The rich bastards for nothing. They have the money and yet here we are living the life. I almost feel sorry for the poor son of a bitch setting in some boardroom worrying about money.

I said, "Jack, do you always get so damned philosophical when drunk?"

He said, "You're not listening. It's all about the swap-off between making all the fucking money or being free to love living life. Are you not as happy as can be? You do not need to answer. I know what you're all about. You showed me who you were when I lowered the boom on Captain Britt England and you could not bring yourself to defend him."

I really didn't like the idea that Jack had my number. I had sold everything I owned to save my soul and buy this boat and this life. I had a little left over to live on and I was going to have to sell a story or two soon to make a few bucks before long if we were to continue this jaunt. Jack knew as much, if not more about where I was than I did. He had figured me out while I wasn't looking.

I was about to defend myself when Jack said, "Enough woman talk. Let's drink and be men. Where's the goddamn food anyway? I'm starving and the women only worry about getting pretty."Jack handed me the bottle. I took a drink and handed it back, quivering inside but done my best not to let it show. Jack turned the bottle up and guzzled a long one, smacking his lips afterwards saying, "Fruit of the goddamn Island Gods."

He wiped his mouth across his forearm and said, "I'm hungry. I thought we were going to eat?

I said, We'll eat when it's time." I looked him in the eye and said, "What did you do before becoming a captain?"

He took another drink of rum and said, 'I wasted my time."

I said, "Wasted it doing what?"

He laughed and pointed out to sea and said, "On a misspent youth and missing out on all this."

He wasn't going to give it away. If I was to learn of his past, I was going to earn every morsel of information. I had caught enough from his rambling about money and freedom to guess there was more to him than met the eye. I also realized he was displeased with himself for letting anything slip. I understood free spirits were born, not created and being one demanded swimming against the current. Jack was one.

Before I could say another word, our late morning breakfast arrived. My island girl came on deck carrying a platter of food fit for a king's feast. She sat it before us and disappeared below to return with a tray of coffee and sweet rolls. I winked at her and said, 'Thank you baby."

Jack looked at the enormous amount of food on the platter and said, "Didn't you make him any?" as he waved a hand my way.

Jack took the coffee pot, poured a cup and then added a healthy spot of rum. He sliced into his steak, blood poured from it mixing with the eggs turning them pink. "Perfect." He said. I poured myself a cup and took my plate. Jack eyed me as I raked eggs into it but he was too busy eating to talk. I took a couple of golden brown conch fritters, a steak and a sweetbread roll and dug in. All I could think is; this is the life.

My Island girl joined us and we ate in silence as The Island Girl gently glided on the sea. The clouds were thinning and the sun painted the sea and the water had returned to blue. I finished my breakfast, gave my island girl a kiss, and said, "Thank you. It was delicious."

She smiled saying, 'Thanks," then jokingly said, "Now you and Jack can do the dishes." She knew it would provoke a rant from Jack.

Jack almost finished chewing the bite in his mouth before he cut loose. "I captain this vessel and will not pull double duty as a galley boy." He swung an evil look at me and said, "Wash dishes if you want galley turd! I'll toss mine overboard and be done with it." I was laughing too hard to answer. That pissed him off even more. He began cursing and bits of food flew from his mouth as he geared-up into a rage.

Jack stood, grabbed his plate and sailed it like a frisbee toward the sea.

My island girl yelled, "That's my grandmother's china!" Jack jumped up and ran to the rail and before the plate had hit water, dove overboard disappearing below the surface. I watched the plate hit and skip like a stone about twenty yards out before beginning to sway back and forth as it sank. We moved to the railing and could see Jack was zeroing in on the plate.

He was a fish in the water. The blue water was so clear that we could see him as he reached out his right hand and the plate settled into his grasp. He must have been fifteen feet below the surface. With a hand on each side, he used the plate like a tailfin to swim upward. As he resurfaced, he held the plate high above his head, shot a long spout of water from his mouth and said, "I have retrieved your heirloom, my lady!"

She looked at me and laughed as she said, "How do I tell him that I bought the set of dishes at a dollar store?"

I let out a big belly laugh and when I was able, I said, "Let's not let him know just yet. This is too good. As of now, he is your hero and champion." She was still laughing and attempting to straighten her act up as I turned the Island Girl to go and retrieve our Captain Jack. He came alongside and climbed back aboard with the dollar store plate.

As Jack made the deck, he shook water like a big fuzzy dog, ran his fingers through his hair in an attempt to gain the proper look to approach a lady. He bowed as he reached out the plate to her and said, "Although it was partially my fault this piece of china was almost lost, I was able to save it for you my lady." He stood as stoic as any man in history awaiting her response.

She looked to me and I smiled as she joined in in the skit playing before us, only I don't think Jack was playing at anything but being Jack. My island girl curtsied, saying, "Jack, you have saved a precious piece of your queen's dowry. Jack bowed before her again as she said, "For this deed, I Knight you," then she took a steak knife and tapped his shoulder three times and said, "Rise, Sir Jack of Cubico.

Jack stood, shoulders pushed broad and took his place at the helm. My island girl came to me and said, 'How did I do with my first act as Queen of Cubico?"

I smiled trying to not laugh aloud and spoil Jack's big event. I said, "You are fitting into his world very well. He wasn't worth shit before, now I fear he will get even worse at being Jack. Being Sir Jack of Cubico, may be too much for him to handle."

Jack didn't say much, but kept walking about inspecting the ship from bow to stern. It was late afternoon before the girls made an appearance. Jack summonsed me to tell them the story of how he became Sir Jack of Cubico. I laid it on thick. "Girls if you could have only seen Jack risk his life by diving into shark infested waters to save one piece of china, well, I have never before seen anything so brave. This man is a true American hero of the sea. We are very lucky to know such a man."

I could never figure if Jack was an actor or really a nut. He did seem to love playing the part, but he made it seem too real to be an act. I did understand having him aboard made life and sailing more interesting, to say the least. At any given moment, he was a pirate, a knight in shining armor, a jerk, a wonderful fisherman with great knowledge of the sea, a drunken idiot, and the best friend one could have.

Jack was a total pain in the ass and yet fun to have around. I guess I liked him more than I wanted to admit. He always brought a fresh and different way of thinking to the table. At times, it was way the hell off the wall but came with some depth that made you think that he may be onto something the rest of us just can't seem to grasp. That was the scary side of him. That was what he had that others feared, and he reveled in it.

As I told the girls of his great feat, they swooned and awed as they slid beneath his arms. He wrapped his arms around them but seemed oblivious to anything other than being Sir Jack of Cubico, Captain of The Island Girl and future Commodore of the Cubican Navy. He said, "Now girls, it's early and we have plenty of time to make Sir Jack a happy Captain. First, we celebrate a minimum of twenty-four hours. It is the proper protocol, you see.

I headed below to my island girl leaving Jack to his whelm, which, as usual, seemed to be all about him. Just before disappearing below, I heard him say, "More rum wenches. Bring 'Ol Jack more rum and quarter a few limes. You're going to taste the marrow of life tonight you sweet wenches. 'Ol Jack is feeling a bit naughty and it's nice so be ready to yell as I plunge to the depths!" They giggled saying, "Oh, Jack. You're bad!"

I was laughing as I found my sweetie. She said, "What's so funny?" I told her about Jack and his plans for the girls. I said, "I'll bet if you told him about the dollar store plate, his pecker would wilt for a month."

She laughed and said, "Now that would not be fair to the girls, would it?"

I said, "The hell with the girls and Jack, I'm more worried about me. What do you think?"

She said, "It's very early in the afternoon to be needing a private audience with your queen. But if you insist, I will allow it." I took her hand and we made way to the master birth. We could see the white of the gulls sailing against the sky through the portholes. Calm water barely moved the vessel as we lay listening to the sounds of the sea. She said, "Being in good with royalty has it perks, huh?"

We relaxed and enjoying the late afternoon as the sun beamed through starboard portholes. The smell of the sea blew lightly across the cabin. Nothing was better than spending time with my island girl while doing nothing other than being happy. I finally got up, struggled my way to the galley and poured us two tall glasses of iced tea. My island girl was setting propped by pillows when I returned.

Every line and curve of her body was sexy and as I handed her her drink, I accidently spilled a little tea from her glass and it splashed on the center on her tummy running like a small creek downward settling into her belly button. The tea was icy cold, she stiffened somewhat and little chill bumps rose on her tummy. I sat my drink on the bedside table, bent down and kissed the chill away.

The sun was setting and the clouds looked bright orange and deep red as we sat watching the day turn to evening using the portholes as our window to the world. If anyone was enjoying life more, I wondered who the hell they could be and what they were doing. The only sounds were of our breathing and small waves lapping against the hull of The Island Girl.

Somewhere in the distance, a dolphin chatted to its mate. My island girl rose slightly upward and said, "We're not the only true lovers this evening," as the dolphins sang love poems back and forth. She looked sexier than ever as little beads of sweat formed in the dimple of her upper lip making her even more sexy. I had never been happier nor wanted her more. We kissed. I tasted the salt on her lip as we again melted within a deepness like night.

We fell asleep in each other's arms. Deep in the night I was awaken by loud noises. My island girl was sleeping with her head on my chest and I didn't want to move. I just lay and listened. It didn't take but a moment to realize Jack was still partying on deck. His big mouth and Jimmy Buffett singing was the noise that woke me. I smiled as the sound of glasses clinking together on deck came with the night through the porthole.

Jack was going to be a bear in the morning no matter how well tonight went. I wasn't worried about him, I had my girl in my arms listening to her soft breaths as she slept and couldn't have cared less if he fell overboard. "He Went To Paris" came over the speakers and I squeezed my island girl tightly as I listened to the words. I knew I didn't want to be that old man at the end of life without my girl beside me.

I loved watching her sleep. Tonight, moonlight angled through an open porthole where it was drawn to her. She looked so calm and happy, almost unreal. I was confident not many men had been so lucky even for a short period, and yet, I had been this lucky over half my life. As she slept, I felt her breath ease across my chest as her head lay upon my shoulder. I smiled, closed my eyes and drifted off.

I awoke to sounds of more dolphin chatter. They seemed to love following The Island Girl. The sun was bright yellow as it arose and the day was on in a good way. I could hear breezes catching the sails like a distant roll of thunder that you weren't sure were real. The ship swayed slightly with the wind rocking in an easy motion that was better than good for a soul. I yawned and looked towards my island girl.

Her tanned skin was smooth creamy chocolate against the white of the bed sheets. She was sleeping peacefully with not a worry in the world. I had lived my life for this day and to see her so happy and content. I was a lucky man to be here and smart enough to realize it. I was also smart enough to know it was more her will than mine that we had survived. She was it and I had always known that. She knew it too.

She had always said that she seen something in me that everyone else had missed. Many times, I'd gone out of my way to screw it up but she didn't give up on me. We were small pawns in a big world filled with all the trappings and yet we somehow had made it through the gauntlet to live on the bluest ocean and with the biggest of smiles each morning. I think the smiles were because we knew we'd beaten the devil at his own game.

I heard bare feet running on deck. Then, I heard Jack gagging and puking. I hoped he'd made it to the railing and was puking overboard. I chuckled and eased out of bed, not wanting to wake my island girl. I slipped into the galley and made coffee. As usual, in minutes, the smell of the fresh coffee brought my girl to life and she joined me in the galley. I kissed her forehead as I handed her a steaming cup.

We sipped our coffee sitting side-by-side. Jack had stopped his awful sounds before my girl awoke and I figured he had either fallen overboard or had just fell dead. My island girl took a last sip and said, "I'm heading to the shower," and she headed off with her brown backside holding my attention as she disappeared. I smiled shaking my head .

I took my second cup of coffee and headed on deck to see if I needed to hire a new Captain. But there was Jack, a beer in his hand and the girls sleeping it off laying nude across deck chairs. He took a swig, looked to them, then back to me, and said, "Sissies. God love them, but they can't party for shit."

I said, "You think we should cover them before anyone else comes on deck?"

Jack said, "Do with them as you please."

The girls hung loose and limp looking as if an explosion had blown them into chairs. The only sign they were alive was slight breathing sounds and a moan now and then. Jack waved an arm their way saying, "Toss them overboard. I cannot abide such a lack of ability."

I said, "Jack, tossing things overboard hasn't worked out real well for you as I recall."

He said, "I beg your pardon. It is Sir Jack of Cubico, to you mate and it seemed to work quite well as I am now almost royalty."

There was no use attempting to argue Jack's logic. He was drunk, but even sober; Jack lived in a world where he was always right. I said, "Jack, are you feeling alright? I thought I heard you barfing earlier."

He smirked tossing the empty bottle into a cooler, pointed to the girls and said, "Such lack of ability to continuously entertain the good spirit of the life made me sick.

I said, They're young. Give them time."

He said, "Let's spend the day fishing?"

I said, 'Let's get the girls below first. They can't be comfortable." I went to get sheets to wrap them before hauling them below. I glanced at them one last time. They were a pair to behold and put together as perfect as nature can and at the moment, presented a mixture of twisted Picasso and Salvador Dali composition that could be titled, "Death on a Drunken Sea." I headed below and took a pair of sheets out of the drawer. I only hoped Jack didn't lose an ear or worse before it was over.

My island girl was out of the shower and asked what I was doing. I told her. She said, "Jack is going to kill those two before it's over."

I said, "Or they will kill him!"

"Would you like some help?" she asked."

I said, "Sure."

She said, "Would you rather I go up and take care of it?"

I said, "I don't mind hauling them down, but I could use the help if you want. They are out cold and will be dead weight"

She said, "I'll bet you don't mind." She giggled saying, "I'll handle it."

I said, "Well, I can help. I'll do it with my eyes closed."

She said, 'You are forgetting, I know you. You won't even squint one eye. I know how sexy they are."

I said, "I won't lie, they are lovely but I have all I can handle."

She laughed and said, "You have more than you can handle."

I said, "Shall we see?"

She said, "Maybe. But let's get the girls below before the day's heat gets them." We headed on deck as humanitarians hell bent on saving a pair of fallen angles.

When we reached the girls she said, "My god, they look terrible." She whirled on Jack and said, "What did you do to them?"

He said, "My Lady, before you are prime examples of youth that never learned to hold their liquor. They are beautiful although somewhat frail in the social graces necessary to sail with Sir Jack," and then he offered her a beer.

She looked at me and said, "Let's get these poor girls below."

Jack said, "Toss them overboard," as he swiped the back of his hand towards the sea. "I'm finished with them! At best, they fall far short of all previous expectations."

My island girl said, "Jack, sit down and shut up!" He picked up a cooler, whirled and took his place at the helm. I heard the spew of a beer being opened as we awoke the girls and all but carried them below. They staggered and stumbled and moaned. We held them upright and herded them towards their births. If zombies ever existed, we had a matched pair on this morning.

After putting them to bed, we stopped in the galley and had more coffee. It gave her time to cool down. I could see she was ready to kill Jack. She said, "You can't agree with how he treats women?"

I said, "Hell, I don't agree with how he treats the world. But I can tell you this, no one is going to change him. He is what he is. Whatever that is. The girls should have known the score when they signed on. He was drunk when he met them. It don't take a rocket surgeon or a brain scientist!" She giggled at my screwed up metaphoric observation.

I stayed with her and in a little while, she settled a bit. It was still very early, we had a full day ahead, and I wasn't going to allow two passed out girls and a drunken captain to rule the day. I said, "Why don't you get your camera and come with me? We'll catch some small fish and feed the dolphins. You should get some really good dolphin photos."

She smiled and said, "Yes, let's make this a good day."

We hit the deck, her in a yellow bikini with a black camera and its long lens extended outward like a pirate's telescope between her breasts as she adjusted the settings. She was a stickler for getting it right and the sunlight reflecting off the sea forced perfection. She said, "Give me a moment, or all I'll get is glare and odd shapes and ghost at the edges of strange shots". Even with fun photography, she wanted it right.

I hung a bag of frozen chum over the side and readied a fly rod with a cream and red fly as she looked for dolphins. The chum drew a crowd rather quickly. I had always been amazed at how pretty the perfect cast of a fly was to the human eye. The line rolls through the air arcing magically to a preplanned location in the same fashion an artist strokes the brush to canvas. We were good.

I seen the water swirl and felt the strike. I ripped the rod upward setting the hook. The rod bowed as I felt the pressure of the fight. One of my favorite things about saltwater fishing was the power of the fish. No matter the size, they stripped line with an unbelievable speed and strength.

Catching them was more than sport; it was what life is about in the deepest crevices of the human mind. I knew in my heart that I felt the same adrenaline rush and racing heartbeat as the first human who caught a fish.

The line cut water in long straight slices, the reel whined, line slipped between my fingers. The tip of the rod thumped, bending deep as the fish shook and dove with uncanny speed. The sky filled with birds swooping to the chum. I could hear the shutter click as my island girl maneuvered to get photographs. I loved the guessing and figuring in what the fish would do next and the pride of being one-step ahead at its every turn.

There is rawness to bringing death and it is unmatched by anything the mind conjures. It is a sad energy without explanation that only nature fully understands. Deciphered, it concludes man can kill and be thrilled with killing but always with slight remorse in knowing, he can be next. The winners and losers in a battle to the death exhibit equal degree of need and with only one champion in the end and there can be no other feeling that comes close for either.

I kept the tension tight enough to tire him without giving what he needed to tear off, or break line. I glanced to my right and Jack was tying a fly and readying to join in. He couldn't tolerate action without being a part of it. I didn't mind the competition, it was a big ocean with plenty of fish. I said, "Get your line wet before you fall too far behind." The challenge had been presented.

The fly rod was an extension of Jack. There was no separating the two. His casts were smooth, sleek and without wasted motion. The bastard was good and he knew it. He was also an ass and enjoyed showing off. With little effort, he sent his fly far past where I had cast just to piss me off. While I was fuming, my fish lunged deep breaking the tippet. It was gone. I was pissed that I had allowed Jack to get to me.

As I was winding line back onto the reel, I glanced toward Jack and he was smirking without looking at me. I knew what he was thinking. I checked my tippet for frays, took a new fly, and tied it, cinching the knot tight. From the corner of my eye, I saw Jack whip the rod-tip upward setting the hook. The fish jumped, climbing on air propelling itself up by flipping its tail. It was small, but it was a fish.

Jack was a pain in the ass but he forced you to be better at everything. He ate away at your armor until you had to look at yourself stripped down and bare-assed. It made me uncomfortable and better at the same time and I didn't like it no matter how much I may have needed it. With Jack, it was never really about what you thought it was about. It was no longer just fishing to feed the dolphins. He had inserted himself into our morning and doing so changed everything. It was still fun but different now.

Viewed righteously, everything was a sport and a competition and losing in any competition should make one's stomach churn to a sickness. Jack knew of this and we were now engaged in battle. My island girl had moved location in an effort to record it. She felt the difference and even if she didn't approve, she understood what was happening. She snapped pictures in quick succession and I could hear the clicks of the camera as she moved about.

As pissed as I was, it wasn't really aimed at Jack, it was more at myself for letting him distract me. He knew what he was doing and I allowed myself to feed into it. I stripped line and began my cast as Jack brought his fish to the boat. I had grown up fishing with a one-dollar wager on the first fish caught, another dollar on the biggest and a dollar for the most during a trip and this morning I was already down a buck.

I have never liked losing at anything. I can accept a loss if I know I had given everything I had and true enough to myself to know, maybe I could have dug deeper and changed it and other times I understood I was out matched and only needed time to get better at whatever I had lost at. I did not take fishing lightly. I enjoyed it with passion and with a love of the sport, which always demanded improvement.

Jack made short work of the little guy. He brought it alongside the boat, lifted it in, unhooked it, and dropped it into the bucket of seawater I had set aside for that purpose. It cut a rusty when it hit the water and sailed out over the lid and flopped like mad on the deck. After a moment, it lay still. I picked it up and put it back in the bucket and it stayed put. It was tired and content to be back in water.

Gulls swooped on the fish and chum. Our lines sailed out among the gulls before hitting the water. The gulls made quick in-air cuts and dives at the colorful flies, several just missed taking a fly from midair. Jack was making beautiful false cast and line was rolling through the air gaining distance with each cast when an unlucky gull nailed his fly in air. Jack set the hook and the great Jack verses seagull battle was on.

When the gull realized he was attached to Jack, he went acrobatically nuts. At this point, most men would have given up on saving his fly, but not Jack. When Jack put pressure on the gull, it charged toward the tallest sails. Not wanting the bird tangled in the sail's riggings, he jerked hard on the line to pull the gull off course. I was laughing too hard to fish so I held up to watch the Jack-fishing for gull action.

Here was Jack, still drunk and in nothing but a pair of shorts and a straw-hat with his head tilted upward staggering around the deck until he stepped back into the bucket with the little fish in it. The sole of his foot hit the dorsal fin spines and he let out a scream as the spines buried into his foot. He fell backwards cursing the world still holding his rod tip upward and keeping good contact with the gull.

Jack had kicked the bucket, tipping it over and the little fish was again flopping around on the deck, as was Jack. The gull slammed into the rigging and wrapped line around everything it got close to. It had short-lined itself and couldn't get a run and go to break the line. The gull had wrapped line around its feet and was cinched hanging upside down flopping like a big white chicken awaiting its plucking. The little fish's gills were quivering as it lay on the hot deck dying.

Jack had mashed the little fish, effectively sending him to the big fishpond in the sky. Jack was sitting bowed forward plucking the broken spines from his foot and looking like the great white ape that first walked upright. I looked from Jack to the bird and neither was in good shape although the gull was behaving better than Jack.

I turned to my island and said, "This morning really went as I had planned!" She was still turning the lens photographing the dying fish as it lay with its skin and scales quickly drying on the hot deck, next to Jack's foot, and bleeding bright red from the gills. She was so into what she was doing that I don't think she even heard what I had said as Jack, still cursing said, "Worry about pictures of that goddamned fish and I'm going to be lucky if I don't get blood poison and loose a foot."

I said, "Look at the bright side; you may end up with a peg foot."

She snapped a few more shots of the fish, then took a different lens from her bag and started shooting pictures of the gull as it hung from the ropes running along the mast. Its wings splayed wide as it stared down awaiting its fate. Hanging from its black beak was the bright red and white feathers of Jack's fly. She worked twisting the lens and stepping to get something right before clicking the shot.

Once she had finished with the gull, she took some shots of Jack. He was still pulling at the spiny barbs in his foot. He grimaced as he attempted to get a hold of the slimy spines. He finally yelled, "Get me the goddamned Gerber tool from the tackle box." I got the tool for him as she kept shooting pictures. With all the pain, sweat, blood and rawness of the scene, I wondered how the pictures would look.

She was rotating around him clicking the shutter as quickly as she had the camera focused. I could only imagine with all the crudeness, there was some magic taking place here. Jack was wet with sweat. His hands were bloody and he had wiped smears of blood across his face while trying to get sweat from his eyes. His eyes were filled with anguish and that dead fish lay flat and bloody and motionless by his side.

The sun was hot and the darkness of brown dried blood next to the red of fresh blood was powerful. The one thing you could not get in a photograph is the odor of the fish and the copper taste of blood's smell as the two mixes together within the heat of a Caribbean day. With any luck, these pictures would have a degree of excellence that anyone seeing them could inhale deeply and know what we knew, when tasting it on their tongues as they swallowed.

Jack pulled the last spine from his foot as she took a picture. I picked the dead fish up. It was dry and stiff and a little blood ran from its gills as I gave it a toss. I looked into the ocean and the fish floated on its side. It rocked on the small waves as a kite dips against a blue sky. We had no fish to feed dolphins and Jack was crippled again. My island girl seemed happy with her work and that was more than good enough.

She went below to download pictures and Jack was cursing as he worked to get the gull down. After several minutes of twirling and slinging ropes, the gull was on its way to the deck. It held still as Jack removed his fly from its beak. He was proud to get the fly back and he carried the gull to stern and sat it on the railing. He yelled, "Let's fish!" I shrugged my shoulders and reached for my fly rod.

Before I could cast, my island girl called from below, "Come look at these," I looked at Jack and said, "I'll be back in a minute."

He said, "Fuck you. I'll fish alone." He popped the cap on a beer as I left the deck. He was an ass but he had a big heart that couldn't be keep hidden. It had not eluded me that he set the big marlin free, even after it had gored him through the leg and now he had just helped the gull to go free.

I knew it had been a good day for her when I glanced at the computer screen. She had captured Jack in chilling realness with teeth gnashing and clamped tightly together. The muscles in his face were taunt etching an outline of hurt. He had blood across his cheek and forehead as sweat poured from his face streaming downward as rivers. His eyes were the gaunt stare of deep hard pain.

He was humped forward; shoulders pulled inward grabbing for his foot and his khaki shorts darkened with sweat and seawater from the bucket. The little fish was lying beside him, tail turned-up and gill plate partially opened with blood oozing from bright red gills as it lay on the deck in a mixture of its own slime and blood. This picture was as real as pain and death gets. I was proud of her.

She clicked through several pictures, but the first was my favorite. Then, she clicked on one she called "White on White on Blue." It was the gull fighting the fishing line as it tangled itself worse. On either side were the pure white sails, in the center, the white gull, feathers splayed, stretched outward and upward like the officer in "Silence of the Lambs." The far background was a pure blue and cloudless sky.

As I looked at this picture, I thought, what a wonderful way to encase tragedy with beauty. I had never before assumed there was more to living and dying than doing it. As I took in the picture, I knew I had been very shallow in my thinking. There was a sweet pureness in the way the gull had accepted its fate. Although in the end it didn't die, it seemed to have understood the rules and it was at peace.

I leaned forward and kissed my island girl on the top of the head. She had accomplished something very special today and I was as proud as if I had done it. Not many men were ever lucky enough to spend life with such a woman. I was amazed that with all her talent and ability, she still chose to be with me. What she had done with a few the clicks of the shutter, I could not do in hundreds of pages of words.

She looked up at me and said, "What do you think?" I said, 'I think they are really good. You should send them to magazines and see if they'll publish them. I think they're that good."

She said, "I don't know. Maybe they are not that good."

I said, "Baby, these are as strong as anything I have ever seen. Someone will grab them up. You made some magic here and that rarely happens for anyone."

I had not written a single word since we had set sail and I guess seeing her creativity tapped the juices in me. I said, "Let's do this as a duo. You have the pictures. I'll write the story and we'll see what happens."

She said, "What would you write?" I looked out the porthole and answered, "Are you kidding me." I said, "Look at all the stories out there riding waves," as I pointed out the porthole to the sea."What you've photographed, really don't need words, but we can sell them better with a story to go with them."

She smiled and said, "Write the words." I was already sketching an outline in my head. I hugged her and promised a story that would do justice to her photographs. I poured a drink and offered it to her. She declined and I took the drink and my laptop and headed on deck. Putting pen to paper had always come easy to me. The difficulty was satisfying myself that I had written it with trueness the reader could touch.

I took a long drink, listened to the ice settle in the tall glass, and began typing with the idea of writing myself into the writing of a story. If it were an easy task, I probably would not write. I liked the challenge of creating on a blank page. It was like making love, you always know when you have done it right, and you know when it was just okay. When you get it right, you want to stand and pound your chest. When you get it just average or worse, gotten it wrong, you want to go to the bar, get drunk and punch a bully in the face.

Writing about Jack should be easy but it wasn't. It was easy if only writing what you see on the surface. But there is a tragedy hidden deep inside him and I'm not sure he even knows it. Beneath a crude rugged exterior, there is something buried that rarely lets out. You have to look hard to ever see it, but it is there. Putting that struggle into words was the job at hand. If I could eke it out, I'd earn my share of the doubloons when we sold the photo-story.

I leaned back, put my hands behind my head interlocking my fingers as Jack walked over and said, "What the fuck?"

I picked up the glass draining it before saying, "Writing a goddamn story."

He took a sip of beer and said, "What kind of goddamn story?"

I sit the glass down and said, "I think it's about that fish and gull."

He said, "Who the fuck wants to read about a goddamn bait fish and bird? Let's get drunk!"

He handed me a beer. It was the noon hour and I thought, why not. I sipped my beer and listened to Jack as he rattled on. 'You know if it was a big fish, I could see writing a story but a goddamn little fucking bait fish and a dumbass gull, just isn't a story there." He had no idea how wrong he was and I just listened to him pile it on as he drank one beer after another. My mind was running one line after another as I listened.

Between beers he said, "Big fish, now there's a million stories in catching big fish. Tell the truth, have you ever heard of anyone making good with little fish stories? Goddamn, let's catch a big fuckin' fish and you can write about that." It was hot as hell and cold drops of water formed on the bottle and ran down dripping on my leg, and felt like ice. I grabbed a notepad off the table and scribbled as he talked.

"Big fish and pretty women, that's what you write about," he said, "And only after the fish have been caught and the women loved. You catch the fish at dawn, followed with a day of sailing and drink and then the night is for loving the ladies. You be sure to write that part. It's the only real things in life that truly count. You follow Jack's recipe and you'll have no regrets when Davey Jones comes to call."

I finished my beer and said, "I got it, Jack," as I started to type. It only took a moment for him to become bored and move off. The idea was to put words on the screen until a story emerged and it appeared an easy task until attempted and then it was all different. The page was the beauty you wanted to hold deep in the night and you were sure you would do or say something to screw it all up before it chanced to happen. I was congratulating myself for scribbling Jack's words on the notepad. He had given me something to work with that was very controversial and would match my island girl's photographs in stark rawness.

Writing, every time, was like making love for the first time. You knew where everything was at, but at first, you were never very sure of exactly when to do what.

The fear of getting it wrong made you work harder to get it right and only reached trueness when you knew the story oozed the same passion you were inserting into it. I looked out to the blue water and a shark fin arose near The Island Girl. The chum had drawn sharks. It moved casually into the current surveying the opportunity. It was going to be a very disappointed shark. I watched it cut through the chum line. It was searching for meat too.

Jack had spied the shark and was rigging a heavy-duty pole with a lure as I attempted to find the flesh I seek among an assortment of words. I quickly decided the story was best written if I let it smolder in my mind a while. I was still putting pictures and words together inside my head and they needed to marinade until tinder and the grill was sizzling. Or maybe I just wanted to join Jack and fish and get drunk?

Jack took his rig and walked to where he and the little fish had bled. The sun-dried blood was dark and crisp and cracked by the sun. Jack poured beer onto the brown blood, let it saturate a moment before dipping his fingers in the bloody beer. He rubbed the mixture on the lure, then stood and cast the lure out and in front of the shark. He said, "He'll love the smell of 'Ol Jack's blood." The shark's tail swirled as he headed to it.

Jack held until the shark struck the bait. That takes coolness. There is an urge to set the hook before feeling the strike when you can see it happening. He held and when the vicious hit occurred, Jack laid into the big shark with all he had setting the hooks deep. The rod bent and the line popped loud as a gunshot when it snapped. The shark came out of the water slinging its head throwing the bait back at Jack.

He stood motionless staring at the scene, then said, "Fuck it," as he took a gaff hook and retrieved the lure. He held it up looking at the deep teeth marks in it. Then he took the line and felt along the length of it to see if he could determine what had caused it to break.

I said, "I hear sharks are strange in that they are the only fish that urinate through their skin."

Jack laughed and said, "Sharks that goddamn big can piss however they want."

I handed him a beer, opened one for myself. We stood looking out to sea in silence. It was much too vast for words and it demanded honor from all. It was bigger than the Rocky Mountains and because most of it was hidden, more mysterious than anything on earth except women. There is a reason the sea is revered as feminine in nature. Men only truly love what they can never understand and can never totally own or control.

After a few moments of tranquility, Jack turned, smiled and said, 'I got my lure back!" I nodded and turned to the racket behind us. My island girl was firing-up the grill. I hadn't noticed it was dinnertime. Life on the sea sweeps time as fast as thoughts come and go. She'd brought up a platter of thick marlin steaks covered in spices and ready for the fire. At the sight of food, my gut let me know I had been ignoring it.

She said, "If you guys will put them on in about ten minutes, I'll go below and make a salad."

Jack and I meandered over and checked out the steaks and said, "I have an idea," as he headed below. He returned with two mangos and a roll of foil. He sliced and diced the mangos then covered the grill with foil and lay slices of mango on it and the steaks atop the mango. He then covered the steaks with more chopped mango.

The meat sizzled on the grill as the aroma of mango, garlic and spices filled the air. When the juices cooked down, Jack poured some of his beer into the mix. Steam arose and it smelled as heaven should smell. Then he splashed three-fingers of Jack Daniels on while smiling like a kid bringing home all A's. He flipped the meat, adding some Cajun seafood mix as he worked. The scent form the grill was superb in all aspects.

My island girl came up with a tropical fruit salad that was a blend of every bright color of the palette. Dinner was quickly becoming art for the tummy and the eye. She placed the salad on the table, disappeared back below to return with a tray of golden sweetbread rolls. Jack looked the feast over and said, "Shouldn't we pour rum in the fruit salad then allow it to age before we dine!"

He didn't phrase it as a question, but as an astonished response to a fact he was certain it had been an oversight on our part. Before anyone could answer, the girls appeared, drawn like sharks by the food, I suspected. They looked a bit better than when we had tucked them in this morning. Jack poured two rum totties calling them medicine and handed each a drink, saying, "Drink it down ladies and all will be well."

They took the medicine, seemed better for it as we gathered around the table, and were filling our plates. Jack proposed a toast to my island girl. "Here is to a precious maiden, the namesake of our vessel and the future Queen of Cubico, and a most wonderful chef," as he bowed to her then chugged his drink then feigned tossing the glass over his shoulder and overboard. He smiled and said, "Ah, not again!"

He said, "I'm sure it is another family heirloom."

My island girl said, "Just as much as the plate."

Jack said, "Never would I stoop to send fine family china to the locker of Davey Jones. It would be uncivilized and I am nothing if not a captain and a gentleman." I kept eating to keep from laughing. Jack was so damned serious at being Jack that I was about to choke on my food.

My island girl said, "My ancestors would be so proud of you, Sir Jack. You have defended my honor and saved the royal china, although it was your fault it needed saving, you did, in the end, show bravery."

Jack swigged rum from a bottle, not taking time to fill the glass and said, "I am always at your beckon call," then he turned up the rum and took a drink before offering the bottle to her.

He looked bewildered as she motioned with her hand that she didn't want rum. He shrugged his shoulders and said, "As you please." He turned to his girls and said, "Come wenches, night is soon to be upon us and we must prepare." My island girl sat with me as we finished our meal. It was peaceful now that Jack and the girls had gone below. Evening on the Caribbean was always worth the wait.

Every evening brings a freshness with the cooler air. The sunsets become slices of oranges and of watermelon, depending on a whelm of Gods and create a remarkable ending to the day. As evening grows, the colors glance from the surface of the sea painting everything tropical. You cannot help becoming consumed. I always find myself with the slightest smile, holding her hand and nodding a thank you, in silence to it all.

We stood at the bow as warm splash from cutting waves cooled us like summer rain. I nudged closer to her liking the feel of her as part of me. She leaned into my chest and I smelled the sweet Caribbean breeze in her hair. We were on our own planet making up the rules, as we wished. There was no one or nothing to stop us from anything. I knew if it ended tomorrow, I have known the true freedom of what real love was.

Jack came back up for something he'd forgotten and I yelled to him to make a course correction. He said, "To where?"

I said, "Set her to the westward. We're now chasing the sunset." He looked at me with a question on his lips but never asked it. This was all about making the sunset last. We had the means and I liked the idea as soon it struck me. We were on island time with nowhere to be other than right here.

My island girl turned and gave me a hug and a kiss and said, "Thank you."

I said, "We both love it. So why not follow and see what happens? And now I give you the world's longest sunset." The Island Girl seemed to know what we wanted as she leaned into her new course. Her sails full as she rode high on the seas, bow dead into the setting sun sailing full out just for us.

The feeling for me was the same as the first day we met. On that day, I wanted to be the most amazing man she had ever met and I still lived to steal her heart and to make her mine. I had always been the rainbow chaser and chasing the sun seemed quite normal to me. I think deep inside she loved my crazy streak. She was the more grounded of us but she had always allowed me to be me and I loved her for it.

We were wet from the splash and warmed by the air as we finally lost our race with the sunset and night came, but we had managed to force it to come more slowly than it had planned. Later Jack reappeared and I asked him to set a course for Trinidad. "He said, "We are on that heading now. We should be there in two days, one if the wind stays with us." I hated it when he read my mind. But that was where we were going when the storm forced us off course, so he didn't have to think hard.

We sat on deck for a time before calling it a night. There is something about the

darkness of the sea at night drawing you deep to it. I think it's the knowledge of knowing how minute you really are that brings it all about. You want to believe it is your world and that you are in control but night on the sea reminds you better. You have what you have and nothing else at all to draw on.

I was hoping the breeze stayed strong and at our back. I knew my island girl was ready to do the town. She'd enjoy the color of being in town and being around someone other than me, Jack and the girls. To tell the truth I was looking forward to a day or two out among the landlubbers myself and I wanted to pick up some new lures and new line. A day or two mingling among the masses has always readied me to get.

She settled into bed and I eased into my little nook with my laptop to write the article. Tonight the writing come easy, sentences rolled from my brain and my fingers tapped the keys. In two hours, I had finished and it was ready to forward. Her photographs told the story. My words were only laces that drew the series of pictures tightly together. She had captured images that in the end needed few words. I was next to her and felt her breaths. The Island Girl swooned as I drifted to sleep.

She was up early and I could hear her milling around. With my eyes still closed, I could tell she was excited with the idea of making port at Trinidad. I lay listening, as she made ready for the day. I didn't want to get up but the sun was shining bright and angled through a porthole into my face. I pinched my eyes tight. All that did was force me more awake. No use protesting, I thought, and grumbled as I got up.

I cursed as I missed getting a foot through the leg of my shorts and I heard her laugh as she came in with a cup of coffee. She handed it to me and said, "What's wrong?"

I said, "My goddamned arms are too short or my legs are too damn long. I'm not sure which one it is, but it's causing me to keep missing the leg hole in my shorts."

She said, "Want me to give you a hand?" I said, Hell no. I'll go naked first."

She said, "It's a beautiful morning. When you get dressed, come and enjoy It with me," then she pranced off. I wrestled my shorts until I won, put on my hat so I didn't have to comb my hair, grabbed my coffee and headed up. Once above, the sun felt good and I felt better. The sea was smooth with small wrinkles when breezes rippled it. The sails fluttered sounding raspy and we moved forward.

When you look out every morning at the same scenery, one may think every day at sea is mostly the same but it's not. How you see it is the difference. Other than avoiding other vessels, you have the freedom to steer as you please, depending on prevailing winds. It is that perception of implied freedom that permits one to either see it as new or as the same and it is never really the same even if you want it to be.

No matter where you are, life happens and you are a part of it happening and it will always be different because of you being there. Life anywhere is like that. Being on the sea makes it a little freer. Being on The Island Girl with Jack, his girls and my island girl is life as different as it gets. Out here, it is easy to see how pirates came to be. On the sea, you choose and it's your choice how life is.

I stood aft with my thoughts, somewhat amazed with what we had done. Three months ago, we owned a house in a little town along a skinny valley squeezed tightly into a community by steep hills in eastern Kentucky. It wasn't a bad way to live. It just wasn't where I intended to die. I wanted to know for myself what was beyond island vacations and salty swims at the beach. My island girl felt it too.

The history of the stock that produced me was European and they arrived in America in 1734. We had been French then German and now American. No one knowing this should be surprised at where I was. We were a rambling people from the beginning and I had never felt more at home than I did today. I glanced forward to my island girl. She smiled and waved. If life was about being happy, we had it nailed.

Jack was at the helm, glassing the horizon. I guessed for signs of Land. I moved forward and asked him if we were close. He said, "Close enough," and handed me the binoculars and pointed the direction I should look. There were a couple of fishing boats visible on the horizon. I nodded when I made them. He said, "Land is not too far, half a day's sail. Maybe less. I want to check them out before getting too close. You never know what they really are until you glass."

He opened a beer but kept the watch as we moved closer. About ten minutes later he put the glasses down and said, "Fishing charters. Fuckers greener than you being ripped off and loving it."

I said, "Kind of like you did me that first morning?"

He said, "Four-hundred and fifty dollars to spend a friggin' day anywhere with me is a bargain."

I said, "That it was, Jack. That it was." He grinned like he'd won a prize.

I said, "By the way Jack, we never did settle on a salary for you. How much do I own you for getting us here alive?"

He said, "I was going to really stick it to your ass when this thing started. But you've allowed me to treat the vessel as my own and didn't say shit about the girls. I've had plenty to eat and drink. Hell you even saved my ass when that marlin speared me. How's three grand a month if I stay on?"

I had grown fond of Jack but didn't want it seem happy with his figure. I frowned saying, "Goddamn, Jack, you think I'm made of money? You almost got yourself killed by that damned marlin which would have left us without a captain and not knowing where we even were, and almost got us killed in a hurricane. Shit, Jack?"

He said, I lived and you lived. That is what a good captain does. He see to it everyone lives."

I said, "And what is this, 'If I stay on shit?'

He smiled and said, "I haven't decided if I'll stay as your captain as of yet."

I said, "What? You think I would even want to hire you as a permanent captain.

He fired back with, "I know how boring this trip would have been with Captain Britt England at the helm and so do you. We'll see after a few days on dry land. I may just stay with you and The Island Girl."

It was an argument I didn't care to continue so I gave him a look and walked off toward my island girl. I said, "You look ready for dry land."

She smiled and said, "Let's do the town tonight!"

I said, "Tonight, the land of Trinidad is yours to do with as you please. It's just over the horizon. I hope Jack has contacted the port to arrange mooring for The Island Girl and I had better go check on that with him."

He must have heard me because he screamed, "You're just digging for a goddamn way to Jew me down. For your information, I called the harbormaster early this morning to let him know our needs and expectations. So get off my ass and write the goddamn check." I doubled over laughing. That really pissed him off. He yelled, "What the fuck is so goddamn funny?"

Once I got to where I could talk, I said, "You shithead."

"You're too nervous over the salary you want to be thinking anything except you have over priced your ass as a Captain. I'm thinking I could hire a native Trinidadian captain for a few pesos compared to your high-dollar ass."

Jack, said, "I will not back off one friggin' dime. Attempt to Jew anymore and the price of my services will increase proportionally."

I said, "So you really do want to swim back to Key West?"

I let it set a moment before I said, "Jack, seriously, I want you to know, I have no intentions of firing you. Your price is fair for the amount of adventure and entertainment that comes with you being captain. However, if you choose to leave The Island Girl, never fear I will replace you at a cheaper rate but I am sure lacking the adventure you freely provided. Anyway, I would like for you to stay on as captain."

He said, "I fucking knew it. You've changed methods in an attempt to soften me up, but still working to Jew."

I said, 'Damn it, Jack, I said your price was fair. What the hell do you want?"

He scratched his head and said, "Three girls with an option to switch them out at every port. And more higher priced rum. I am not rotting my gut on the cheap shit you've been serving. That's the deal. Take it or leave it."

I said, "Jack, you drive a hard bargain, but your terms are acceptable."

He said, 'Goddamnit, I knew I could have gotten more. Well, I'll know better next time. A deal is a deal and Ol' Jack never goes back on his word, so If I choose to accept your offer and continue as captain of The Island Girl, I'll let you know, and I will keep my word on that."

He went on to say, "Now, if you would be so generous as to anti-up for my past services so I can enjoy life at port, I would be very grateful. You are aware that selecting the next three will not be an inexpensive outing. There is a substantial cost to holding auditions. I intend to be much more particular than usual and that is always a pricey endeavor." I nodded in agreement, as I counted hundred dollar bills from the ship's cashbox. I said, "You're breaking me up."

He said, "Women are worth it!"

I handed him the cash and being Jack, he recounted it. I shook my head and headed above.

My island girl had gone below to get ready for the evening. I watched ahead as land instead of the sea became the horizon. Just as the long rows of waves became long streamers like contrails as they became breakers rolling toward the beaches, she rejoined me at the bow. She was dressed in the bright color of the islands and looked as pretty as an island princess. Her smiles grew larger as we sailed closer.

We could see many boats and the tall ships with mast of full sails were like fat ghost, free-floating on our sea. We stood together as land formed into bright colors. It looked as if they had painted it just for us. We could do nothing to speed it up and that caused it to be more intriguing. A few aircraft circled, filled with sightseers and vacationers and I felt somewhat bad for them.

I'm sure it is a beautiful sight from the air, but zipping in at two-hundred miles per hour certainly steals away the mystique of wonderment that sailing slowly in holds. We were feeling the moment. She squeezed my hand tightly as a coastline came to life. It was late enough in the day for the little town to be bustling. From here, it seemed the big money box stores hadn't found the way to this small village yet or they were very well hidden from sight. I hoped they were not here.

From afar, it had a look of coastal town where mom and pop were the big business. We anchored a few hundred yards from shore and a small dinghy came to get us. I helped my island girl into the dinghy and Jack herded his girls over the side of The Island Girl. He was last in and he gave our vessel the once over before shoving off. The little boat chopped at the waves bouncing us as we motored in.

The landing was old and wooden and a short climb up. The buildings were more huts than anything else. A Street ran along the beachfront and it was filled with natives selling their goods. The men were barefooted and in khaki shorts and faded Hawaiian shirts. The women were wearing dresses of lightweight bright colored silk like wraps and many women had bright colored head wraps covering their hair. Against the standard tan of the huts, everything was island bright and inviting.

We were deciding what we wanted to do first and must have been taking too long because Jack said, "I'm off to do my bidding," as he and the girls headed into town. I hugged my island girl and said, "Wonder if we'll ever see him again?"

She said, "What are you talking about?" I told her about the chat I'd had with Jack. She said, "We'll see him again. It may not be as our captain, but we certainly will meet on some island somewhere. Jack will always be near the sea and show up when least expected."

We watched Jack walk away with one of his girls on each arm and we both chuckled at the sight. We turned and went the opposite direction towards the market. She said, "Lets buy something new to wear and get a room." She looked deep into my eyes, and said, "I want to break Trinidad in in the proper fashion."

I took the hint, and hugged her tightly and said, "You bet, lady!"

We walked easily and slowly through the heat to the open market area, her underneath my arm, head on my shoulder. The sounds of the street were native and erotic and I knew she was right. We were going to do nothing we didn't want to do and every moment would be something we'd have with us forever and all because she had believed in me and believed in dreams.

90027608R00102

Made in the USA
Columbia, SC
06 March 2018